Books by Shirleen Davies

Historical Western Romance Series

Redemption Mountain

Redemption's Edge, Book One
Wildfire Creek, Book Two
Sunrise Ridge, Book Three
Dixie Moon, Book Four
Survivor Pass, Book Five
Promise Trail, Book Six
Deep River, Book Seven
Courage Canyon, Book Eight
Forsaken Falls, Book Nine
Solitude Gorge, Book Ten
Rogue Rapids, Book Eleven
Angel Peak, Book Twelve
Restless Wind, Book Thirteen
Storm Summit, Book Fourteen
Mystery Mesa, Book Fifteen
Thunder Valley, Book Sixteen
A Very Splendor Christmas, Book Seventeen, Coming Next
in the Series!

MacLarens of Boundary Mountain

Colin's Quest, Book One,
Brodie's Gamble, Book Two
Quinn's Honor, Book Three

Sam's Legacy, Book Four
Heather's Choice, Book Five
Nate's Destiny, Book Six
Blaine's Wager, Book Seven
Fletcher's Pride, Book Eight
Bay's Desire, Book Nine
Cam's Hope, Book Ten

MacLarens of Fire Mountain

Tougher than the Rest, Book One
Faster than the Rest, Book Two
Harder than the Rest, Book Three
Stronger than the Rest, Book Four
Deadlier than the Rest, Book Five
Wilder than the Rest, Book Six

Romantic Suspense

Eternal Brethren, Military Romantic Suspense

Steadfast, Book One
Shattered, Book Two
Haunted, Book Three
Untamed, Book Four
Devoted, Book Five
Faithful, Book Six
Exposed, Book Seven
Undaunted, Book Eight
Resolute, Book Nine
Unspoken, Book Ten, Coming Next in the Series!

Peregrine Bay, Romantic Suspense

Reclaiming Love, Book One
Our Kind of Love, Book Two
Edge of Love, Book Three, Coming Next in the Series!

Contemporary Romance Series

MacLarens of Fire Mountain

Second Summer, Book One
Hard Landing, Book Two
One More Day, Book Three
All Your Nights, Book Four
Always Love You, Book Five
Hearts Don't Lie, Book Six
No Getting Over You, Book Seven
'Til the Sun Comes Up, Book Eight
Foolish Heart, Book Nine

Macklin's of Burnt River

Thorn's Journey
Del's Choice
Boone's Surrender

The best way to stay in touch is to subscribe to my newsletter. Go to https://www.shirleendavies.com/ and subscribe in the box at the top of the right column that asks for your email. You'll be notified of new books before they are released, have chances to win great prizes, and receive other subscriber-only specials.

Thunder Valley

Redemption Mountain Historical Western Romance Series

SHIRLEEN DAVIES

Book Sixteen in the Redemption Mountain Historical Western Romance Series

Avalanche Ranch Press, LLC
PO Box 12618
Prescott, AZ 86304

Thunder Valley is a work of fiction. Names, characters, places, and incidents are either products of the author's imagination or used fictitiously. Any resemblance to actual events, locales, or persons, living or dead, is wholly coincidental.

Book design and conversions by Joseph Murray at 3rdplanetpublishing.com

Cover design by Jaycee DeLorenzo at Sweet 'N Spicy Designs

ISBN: 978-1-947680-31-9

I care about quality, so if you find an error, please contact me via email at shirleen@shirleendavies.com

Description

A frontier lawman, the woman he let slip away,
a sinister threat to her life,
and a second chance neither saw coming.

Thunder Valley, Book Sixteen, Redemption Mountain Historical Western Romance Series

Ezekiel Boudreaux is caught between two worlds. As a deputy in Splendor, Montana, he's an exceptional lawman, able to face down the worst criminals. Underneath, in a place no one ever sees, he hides a soul-deep sense of failure and regret which keeps him from snatching happiness with the woman he's come to love.

Francesca O'Reilly loves the frontier town she now calls home. Her law practice is growing, along with her many friendships. Frannie's one regret is the loss of the man she loves. After months of courting, he walked away, leaving her confused at his abrupt departure and lack of explanation. For Frannie, their time apart hasn't lessened the emptiness in her heart.

Zeke yearns for the same fulfillment his brother has found in his marriage. Struggling to accept the failures of his past, he fights to reclaim Frannie's trust while battling multiple threats to the town and those he cares about.

Working together, Zeke and Frannie sift through clues to identify those responsible for the attacks. Will their efforts unmask those behind the threats, or will time run out, increasing the danger to their town while pushing them further apart?

Thunder Valley, book sixteen in the Redemption Mountain historical western romance series, is a full-length novel with an HEA and no cliffhanger.

Visit my website for a list of characters for each series.
http://www.shirleendavies.com/character-list.html

Thunder Valley

Prologue

New York City
August 1870

"Frannie. You do not have to do this." Nancy Rucker, Francesca O'Reilly's best friend, tried to remove clothes from the satchel faster than Frannie tossed them inside. "Edmund is a fool. He's the one who should leave, not you."

Whirling on Nancy, she crossed her arms. "He broke our engagement, and has announced his intent to marry someone else. I refuse to stay so he can gloat."

"Gloat? Do you know his fiancée?"

"We've met a few times." Dropping her arms, she continued removing clothes from the wardrobe.

"She's a little slow, finds it hard to carry on a basic conversation, and her voice."

Francesca lowered herself to the edge of the bed. "What about her voice?" Although she already understood.

"She, well…squeaks. I know she can't help it. It's why she's almost thirty and still unmarried." Nancy grabbed two chemises, placing them on her dresser. "I do like her, though. She's sweet and generous."

"Perhaps those are the reasons Edmund fell in love with her."

Waving a hand in the air, she sat next to Francesca. "Love? It's the family wealth he's after. I know you come from money, but they make us appear as paupers."

Francesca wanted to dislike the woman. She didn't. All she felt was the sting of humiliation and searing loss. Not so much for Edmund. Francesca refused to think of the real reason for her agony.

Feeling Nancy's hand close over hers, she looked up. "I'm sorry, Frannie. I know why you feel leaving is the best solution. And I hate you're going alone."

"You do remember there are four other women traveling with me? All of us are friends of Rachel Pelletier."

"But you're not good friends with any of them, and it's such a long trip. I should be going with you, Frannie."

Squeezing Nancy's hand, she continued her packing, feeling the weight of all she'd be leaving behind. Most of all, Nancy.

In her heart, Francesca knew going west was the right decision. When her good friend, Rachel, left to join her uncle as a nurse in his clinic, she'd been tempted to accompany her, see the frontier with her own eyes.

She couldn't ignore the opportunity to leave now. Her parents were in good health, with enough money to last several lifetimes. The shock of Edmund's decision to end their engagement impacted them almost as much as it did her. They'd loved him as if he were already a son. A few cruel words from Edmund had ended her vision of a future. The time had come to build another one.

"Do you have time to accompany me to the depot?"

Walking to her, Nancy wrapped her best friend in her arms. "You don't have to ask, Frannie. I'll stay until the train is out of sight."

Chapter One

Splendor, Montana Territory
September 1871

The crack of rifle fire, followed by the bang of six-shooters, sounded through Francesca's office window. It didn't happen often, but each time, the sharp sounds of drunken cowboys or card players shooting out their differences made her jump. Or, as she'd come to understand, when an irate wife found her husband in the wrong bed.

Her profession in the growing town of Splendor offered unending opportunities to be shocked. As a lawyer, she acted as counselor, negotiator, and sometimes a shoulder to cry on. After a year in Splendor, she'd handled property sales, wills and trusts, and divorces.

When Francesca first decided to become a lawyer, she'd applied at The College of William and Mary in Virginia, receiving gracious, yet firm rejections. Her parents reminded her she was younger than many applicants, a woman, and without a sponsor.

Being driven, she'd queried one lawyer after another, seeking someone to act as mentor. In time, they might agree to make a recommendation to William and Mary. Many days of walking and endless conversations,

Francesca found an older man with an established law firm.

Having two male apprentices, she'd been relegated to the role of secretary. Instead of wallowing in disappointment, Francesca sought all possible opportunities to learn. Her grasp of English was impeccable. The innate talent, coupled with excelling in her classes, meant the men gave her enough work for three secretaries. She'd handled each assignment with exacting attention to detail and gracious aplomb, not expecting or receiving credit or extra payment.

What she obtained in knowledge meant more to her than extra coins. After a few years and no longer encumbered with a fiancé, Francesca took everything she'd learned, as well as a letter of introduction, and left for Montana.

Walking to the window, she looked out to Frontier Street, the main road through Splendor. At this time of evening, light came from lamps inside the boardinghouse, saloons, hotel, and restaurants.

She could see the silhouettes of four men in the middle of the street. Two against two. Whoever fired the rifle had set it aside. All four held six-shooters aimed at their adversaries.

Wanting to do something, she grabbed her wrap and ran down the stairs to the street. Few people were stupid enough to stand on the boardwalk when men squared off against each other. Yet here she was, a target for a stray bullet.

Movement down the boardwalk caught her attention. Eyes adjusting, her body stiffened and she looked away. Deputies Zeke Boudreaux and Hawke DeBell stood on the edge of the street, hands resting on their six-shooters.

"No one's going to die on the street tonight, boys. Drop your guns so we can straighten this out." Zeke took decisive steps toward two of the men, leaving the gun in its holster.

Hawke stalked toward the other pair, his gaze focused on the weapons in their hands. "Drop your guns and we'll talk this out."

"To hell we will. Those men have been cheating at cards for months, Hawke. We finally caught them in the act."

He studied the man's face, recognizing the lanky cowboy. "'Evening, Hap. They might well be cheating, but it isn't your job to dole out the justice. Drop your guns, and round up a few more witnesses. If we find there's reason to hold them in jail, we will."

Zeke approached the others, saying the same as Hawke. None of the four budged or lowered their weapons. "Is that you, Herb?"

"It's me, Zeke." Herb worked a few days a week at the lumber mill.

"What's your story?"

"You know I'm not a cheater, and neither is Ralph. Hap's had too much to drink. Ask Nick Barnett. He was watching our game." Herb mentioned the owner of the

Dixie, one of three saloons in Splendor. Four, if you counted Ruby's Grand Palace.

"Good evening, Zeke." Nick walked toward him, his six-shooter secure in its holster.

"Hap and Benny are saying Herb and Ralph are cheating. Anything to add?"

Stroking his gray-tinged mustache, Nick shook his head. "Can't say that I've ever seen them cheating. If I had, they wouldn't be allowed in the Dixie or the Wild Rose."

"That ain't true, Nick. Ralph is real good at it, but he's been cheating a long time. Ask the others." Hap hitched his thumb toward the men standing outside the Dixie.

Nick took cautious steps toward him, keeping his hands loose at his sides. "You and Herb have had a running feud since I moved to Splendor. Are you sure this isn't part of the ongoing grudge?"

"We ain't got a feud," Herb shouted from a few feet away. "Hap's being his usual ornery self."

"I ain't ornery," Hap yelled back, hands fisting at his sides.

While Nick acted as referee, Zeke and Hawke stayed close by, waiting for the argument to wind down so they could take the men's six-shooters.

Francesca inched her way closer, skirting along the side of the buildings, her attention on Zeke. For a time in the spring and early summer, he'd made all the moves of a man interested in courting her.

They'd taken rides, gone on walks, shared more than one picnic, each time growing closer. He'd never used the words, yet all the signals were there.

During that time, she'd become good friends with Christina Boudreaux, Hex's wife. The four had supper together several times, deepening their friendship. She'd been wrong about everything.

Francesca had been shaken when Zeke lost interest, not stopping by her office, not inviting her to lunch or supper, or for long rides out of town. It had been a simple and effective break. He simply disappeared from her life. Months had passed since sharing time with him, yet the pain still felt fresh.

She moved as far as McCall's, a small restaurant close to the jail, watching Zeke and the activity in the street. He hadn't noticed her, which was what she wanted.

First Edmund, and then Zeke. Two men she'd grown to care about. Both shoving her aside when they'd lost interest. At least Edmund had the courage to break off their engagement to her face.

She'd received two letters from her former fiancé over the last month. Edmund wanted Francesca to know he'd ended his commitment to the sweet, quiet woman he'd left her to marry. He'd mentioned nothing about a reconciliation with her, which she'd never consider. Francesca had torn up both letters after one reading, uninterested in anything concerning Edmund or his life.

Paying little attention to the continuing argument, she began moving back toward her office. She'd covered a few yards when a shot rang out, whizzing past her head. A scream left her lips at the same time she picked up her skirts to run.

Pulling his weapon, Zeke's gaze flew to Francesca, heart stuttering at how close Benny's bullet came to her head. Cursing, he helped Hawke take down the drunken cowboy, who continued to wave his six-shooter in the air, while Nick took the guns from Hap, Herb, and Ralph. He helped Hawke escort them to the jail, allowing Zeke to rush after Francesca.

Halfway up the stairs to her office, the sound of the front door opening halted her steps. She gasped, seeing Zeke in the doorway, gun by his side.

Breath faltering from the fact she'd almost been shot, and maybe Zeke's nearness, she straightened her spine, clasping her hands together. Taking the stairs two at a time, he stopped inches from her face.

"Do you want to tell me why you were on the boardwalk while four drunk men threatened each other in the street?"

Lifting her chin, Francesca glared at him. "It's not really your business, Deputy." Turning away, she continued upstairs to his muttered curse, following her.

"Francesca. You almost got shot."

Opening the door to her office, she blocked his attempt to walk in behind her. "That's true." Backing away, she closed the door in his face, leaning against it.

A couple minutes passed before she shoved away, heading straight to her desk. A moment later, Zeke turned the knob and joined her.

"This is serious, Frannie."

Crossing her arms, she lifted a brow. "Francesca."

"What?"

"My name. It's Francesca. Fran and Frannie are reserved for friends." She felt a tiny amount of satisfaction when he winced. "I have a contract to review before going home, so..." Using a hand in a shooing motion, she returned to her office door. "It's time for you to go."

He didn't budge. "We need to talk."

"No, we don't. Please, Zeke, I have work to do."

Taking a step toward her, he rubbed the back of his neck. "I, uh..."

When he said no more, she again motioned for him to leave. "Goodnight, Zeke. I hear Ruby has a new girl at the Grand Palace. Her name is Beauty. You may want to stop by."

Arm dropping, he pinned her with a glare. "What does that mean?"

Releasing an uneven breath, she shook her head. "Nothing. I shouldn't have said anything. Just...please, leave."

Zeke noticed a flash of pain before she hid it. "I'll come by tomorrow to see how you're doing."

Pressing her lips together, she offered a small smile. "You don't need to, Deputy Boudreaux. I have a great deal of work and won't have time to talk."

Studying her face, he ignored the ache in his chest, and sadness in her eyes. Touching the brim of his hat, he gave a reluctant nod.

"No more standing on the boardwalk during a possible shootout."

"I'll make no promises."

Closing the door behind him, Francesca walked back to her chair, slumping into it. Pressing a hand against her forehead, she stared at the work on her desk.

Five minutes later, she continued to stare, unable to keep her thoughts off Zeke. There'd be no concentrating tonight. Giving up, Francesca allowed herself to think about the two times he'd kissed her.

The first time had been after he'd taken her on a picnic to a nearby lake. They'd talked, laughed, shared thoughts as well as their dreams. It had been the perfect day. Before heading back to town, Zeke tugged her to him, brushing a kiss over her lips. One perfect kiss.

The second had been a week later. He'd taken her to supper at the Eagle's Nest in the St. James Hotel. Afterward, he'd taken her hand, guiding her along the boardwalk, then turned toward the house she rented from Noah Brandt. Slipping to a dark area between two buildings, he'd wrapped both arms around her. This one had been longer, more intense, creating flutters in her stomach, a sensation she'd never felt with Edmund.

It, too, had been perfect. Reflecting back, Francesca accepted it hadn't been so perfect for him. Zeke hadn't sought her out again. No more picnics, walks, suppers, or rides.

As with Edmund, she hadn't been good enough for the handsome deputy she'd come to care about. Tonight had been the first time he'd done more than tip his hat. A gesture he offered to all women in town. Polite and impersonal.

Shoving out of her chair, she extinguished the light on her desk. Tomorrow was another day, one which wouldn't include Deputy Boudreaux.

Chapter Two

"Well, well. We haven't seen you in a while, Deputy Boudreaux." Ruby Walsh, resplendent in an emerald green silk dress embellished with black lace, took the chair next to Zeke, motioning for the waitress. "We'll have a couple whiskeys, Beauty."

The slender, ethereal looking waitress, with long white-blonde hair, and silver gray eyes, let her gaze move over Zeke before offering a wan smile.

"Beauty, this is Deputy Zeke Boudreaux. Zeke, one of the newest girls, Beauty."

"It's a pleasure, Beauty."

Her head dipped in his direction. "Deputy."

Ruby waved her off. "You can get those drinks now."

"Yes, ma'am." She turned away, but not before another appreciative gaze slid over Zeke.

"Beauty is older than she appears. She told me her age is nineteen, but I'd wager it closer to twenty-three. No family to speak of. She's been here a few months, but as I said, you haven't been around in quite a spell."

"Here you are." Setting down the whiskeys, Beauty lingered a few seconds before Ruby motioned for her to leave them alone.

"She has a lilt to her voice. Where's she from?"

"Ireland, traveling here with her family when she was about seven. All but an aunt died on the boat from a fever. Beauty lived with her until she passed a few years ago. Hence..." Ruby waved her arm over the tables in the Palace, "her move into my world." Picking up her glass, she tipped it toward Zeke.

Sipping his whiskey, he studied Beauty, who stood at one end of the bar. "What brought her to Splendor?"

"Why? Are you interested?"

An image of Francesca, her wavy auburn hair, green eyes, and smile that would light up his world for days, settled in his mind. "No. Just curious."

Ruby emptied her glass, setting it on the table. "Honestly, I don't know. She's one of the most private women I've ever met. It took a good deal of work to learn what I told you." Shifting in her chair, she studied him as one would an unknown creature. "What are you doing in here, Zeke? It's obvious you have no interest in the entertainment we offer."

Picking up his empty glass, he held it up, rolling it between his fingers. "Taking some time for myself, Ruby. Nothing more."

A knowing grin curved her lips. "All right, Zeke." Setting her hands on the table, she stood. "Should I send Beauty over with another drink?"

"One more whiskey. Thanks, Ruby."

Leaning back, Zeke stretched out both legs, his thoughts going to Francesca. Almost three months had gone by since he'd been within touching distance of her. It had taken all his self-control not to take her hand in his and kiss each finger before folding her in his arms.

She'd made it clear he no longer had the right to consider her a friend. He'd lost the privilege when he'd made the decision to slow their courtship. His decision, not hers, and one he'd intended to explain.

One week, two, then a month passed as he struggled with how to tell Francesca he wasn't ready to commit. It was a lie. The truth was he didn't deserve a woman as cultured, smart, educated, and accomplished as Francesca. Funny and compassionate, she was all he could ever hope for.

As for him, Zeke knew his numbers and could read when needed. He'd served in the Confederate Army and been a lawman. The sum of his life in a few words. He convinced himself backing away would save her for a man worthy of such a woman. Being near her today, the doubts crept in, making him wonder if the decision had been the right one.

The impact of his silence had been clear in her words. She couldn't stand to be near him, didn't want to see or talk to him. He couldn't blame her.

Hurting Francesca had never been his intention. Regret whirled through him. Being unable to find the right words, not going to her to explain in person, had cost both of them a great deal.

Finishing the last of his whiskey, Zeke walked outside. The late night air felt cool compared to the stuffy interior of the Palace. Before going home in a few hours, he needed to relieve another deputy.

The excitement caused by the four angry cowboys had long ago worn off. They now slept their drunkenness off in jail, Hawke guarding them. Shane Banderas, another deputy, would be making rounds until Zeke took over.

He looked forward to it. Walking would give him time to think, clear his head of Francesca's image, and help him figure a way to make amends.

"It's Saturday night, meaning men from the Devil Dancer Gold Mine will be coming to town." Gabe Evans, the sheriff of Splendor, and one of the leading businessmen, stared at the bored faces of his deputies.

"It's the same every Saturday, Gabe. Something different about this one?" Cash Coulter, a good friend of Gabe, and one of the first deputies hired, leaned back in his chair, cleaning his fingernails. Known to carry a Bowie knife, today, he used a shorter Mansfield/Lamb fighting knife.

"It's always the same," Beau Davis, another friend and original deputy, added. "They get paid, drink too much, lose money at cards, then fall asleep behind one of the buildings."

"Unless they keep enough money to find solace in one of Ruby's upstairs rooms," Mack Mackie added to the chuckles of others.

Holding up a hand, Gabe silenced them. "The difference tonight is the owners of the Angel Wings Silver Mine are handing out their first payroll." He didn't have to explain what that meant for them.

A chorus of groans came from his men. Most were former Union or Confederate soldiers, some ex-Texas Rangers. All experienced and used to hard work.

Splendor's growth allowed him to hire nine men and one woman, his brother Chan's wife, Beth. He'd match each deputy against two from anywhere else. With the increase in townsfolk, number of large ranches, gold mine, silver mine, and a new copper mine hiring, he could use another half dozen.

"The miners won't be arriving in town until about five. We can go with Mack, Hex, and Caleb between now and then. I'll need the rest of you tonight."

The others didn't argue. The three Gabe mentioned were married with young children.

"If we're lucky, the men will go through their money and leave for the mines by midnight. I'll be with you tonight."

Dutch McFarlin, a former Pinkerton detective, gave a decisive shake of his head. "No need for you to be here, Gabe. You and Lena have baby Emma at home. We can take care of tonight."

The others nodded or voiced their agreement.

"I'll wait to see how many men arrive from the mines. Remember, the ranch hands from the Pelletier and other ranches will be celebrating a Saturday night with everyone else. I prefer too many deputies than too few."

Shoving out of his chair, Gabe grabbed his hat, settling it on his head. "I'm heading out to talk with Nick and Noah. Everyone except Mack, Hex, and Caleb, go home. See you this evening."

Zeke walked outside with his brother, Hex, both taking a few steps before stopping to look around. It had been three days since Zeke had seen Francesca, and he still didn't know how to approach her again.

"How are the girls?"

A slow grin appeared on Hex's face. "Happy, which is usual for Lucy and Cici. Marrying Chrissy was the best decision I ever made."

A quick pang of envy shot through him before Zeke thrust it away. "You deserve finding happiness, Hex."

"Francesca came to supper last night." He let that hang between them.

Zeke didn't know how to respond without giving away his deep regret.

"She and Chrissy talked a long time after supper." Hex looked into the distance. "I've never asked, but what happened between you two?"

Zeke swallowed, feeling his Adam's apple bob as he struggled to decide what to say.

"Never mind. It's not my business."

He wanted to laugh at his brother's comment. They were close. Blood kin and good friends who relied on each other for most of their lives. After returning to New

Orleans after the war, they'd done their best to revive the failing family business without success. It had been in decline too long.

Together, they'd made the decision to sell, leaving the city of their birth to head west. Their destination had been a mystery as they crossed the border of Louisiana and rode into Texas.

After months of traveling, working when needed, they'd landed in a saloon in the Montana territorial capital of Big Pine. Two deputies from Splendor were also there. Over a few beers, they explained the town's need for more deputies, suggesting the brothers take the day's ride west to learn more.

Together, he and Hex had made the decision to take them up on their offer to meet Gabe Evans, the sheriff. And together, the brothers decided to accept positions as deputies in the growing frontier town.

Zeke hooked his thumbs into his belt. "I made a mistake with Francesca."

Brows bunching together, Hex shifted his gaze from down the street to his brother. "Courting her?"

"She's sophisticated, educated. Hell, she's a lawyer. Gabe and his family use her. So do the Pelletiers and Brandts."

"Are you implying you're not good enough for Frannie? If that's so, I'm certain she wouldn't agree."

Zeke thought of her biting words a few nights before, the hurt etched on her face. The way his failure to explain himself ended whatever had been growing between them. Whether good enough for her or not, she would never give him another chance.

"Doesn't matter." Saying nothing more, Zeke clasped his brother on the shoulder, leaving Hex to stare after him.

Stomach growling, he headed across the street, walking toward the boardinghouse restaurant. He would've preferred McCall's this morning. Quieter, with fewer people this time of day. It was located next door to Francesca's office, a place he'd made the decision to avoid for the time being.

After a spell, he'd return for breakfast and evening supper, times Francesca would normally be home. The one bedroom house she rented from Noah and Abby Brandt was a couple down from where Chrissy and Hex lived. Meaning, he had to walk right past it with each visit to his brother's. He hoped the unease would disappear in time.

Passing the Assay Office, he prepared to open the boardinghouse door when a high-pitched scream drew his attention. Whirling around, hand on the handle of his six-shooter, he began running in the opposite direction.

"Help!" Two women stood between the land office and the Dixie, faces pale, one of them pointing toward the opening between the two buildings.

Zeke reached the scene at the same time as Caleb and Mack, guns drawn, moving between the women and whatever caused their distress. The sight before them had all three turning away, trying not to retch.

A body, covered in blood, lay crumbled on the ground, a Bowie knife protruding from the center of his neck.

Chapter Three

Zeke motioned toward Caleb and Mack before kneeling next to the body. "Caleb, get the women away from here. Mack. Fetch Doc McCord."

The man's clothes were covered in blood, and dirt, as if he'd tried to crawl away from his attacker. Glancing behind him, Zeke saw what appeared to be scuffle marks in the dirt.

The Bowie knife drew his attention. Typical of the weapon, the blade was about nineteen inches long. The handle protruded from the front of the man's neck, the blade piercing through the back. If he'd already eaten breakfast, he knew the food would now be on the ground beside him.

Zeke had witnessed sabre wounds during the war. Never had he seen this extreme brutality to a civilian with the sharp, lethal knife.

"Who is he?" Gabe ran up, kneeling next to the body.

Jaw clenched, Zeke rose to face Gabe. "I don't recognize him. Do you?"

"No, but that doesn't mean much with the way the town is growing." Gabe's eyes locked on the knife, bending down to study the man's face. "No bruises or scrapes." Picking up a hand, he turned it over before doing the same to the other hand. "Nothing to indicate he tried to defend himself." Straightening, he took in the rest of the body. "The only visible wound is the killing strike made with the knife. He knew the person who did this to him. But why would the killer leave such a recognizable weapon?"

"I'm thinking he must have been interrupted," Zeke answered. "No one would leave a knife as valuable as this unless necessary."

"Has someone gone for Doc McCord?"

"Mack's getting him."

"Gentlemen." Nick's gaze landed on the dead body.

Gabe shifted to give his friend and business partner a better view. "Ever seen him before, Nick?"

"Yes. Name's Harmon Tibbs. He owns a small ranch east of town. Comes into the Dixie early on Fridays for supplies. Stays to play cards before heading back."

"Did you see him leave with anyone last night?"

"No. I'll ask Paul. Maybe he saw something."

"Where is he?" Doctor Clay McCord pushed through the small crowd, kneeling next to the body, groaning at the gruesome sight. Recovering, he glanced at Gabe. "Isn't this Harmon Tibbs?"

"Nick recognized him," Gabe answered. "Was he one of your patients?"

"Saw him once a couple months back. He didn't deserve this." Sighing, Clay stood. "I'll talk to the undertaker. Let me know if there's anything I can do, Gabe. We can't let his killer get away with this."

Zeke had said nothing after Nick walked up and Doc joined them. He'd thought the man a drifter, not a local rancher.

"What do you want me to do, Gabe?" Zeke asked.

"Wait until the undertaker arrives for the body, then start questioning anyone in the Dixie last night. I also want to know who else in town carries a Bowie knife. Speak to the business owners on Frontier Street. One of them may have seen something."

Zeke looked down at the body, wincing at the gruesome sight. "Why would the killer leave it behind? There has to be someone who'll recognize it."

"I'll speak with Cash. He might've noticed someone with a knife similar to his. Mack and Caleb will be talking to people and business owners east of Palace Street." Gabe scrubbed a hand along the stubble on his jaw. "I'm going to send a telegram to Sheriff Parker Sterling in Big Pine."

Watching him leave, Zeke walked the few steps to the boardwalk, taking a slow perusal of the street. He recognized most of those standing around, and the drivers of several wagons. A few stared at him, but didn't approach. No doubt they'd heard about the body and were keeping their distance.

His gaze jerked to a stop on a beautiful woman with auburn hair coming out of McCall's. Francesca, a broad smile brightening her face. Right behind her was a tall man wearing a suit, top hat, and polished boots, a broad hand at the small of her back before she slipped her arm through his.

A knot formed in Zeke's stomach, fury tightening his chest. He had no right to feel any reaction at her being with another man.

When they disappeared through the front door of her office building, he tried to convince himself the man was a client who'd retained Francesca as his lawyer. Crossing the street, he walked straight into McCall's, taking a seat at an empty table by the front window.

"Haven't seen you in a while, Zeke." Betts set down a cup of coffee. "What can I get you?"

"Just coffee for now."

She filled his cup, and started to turn away before he picked it up, holding it to his lips.

"I saw Miss O'Reilly leave here a few minutes ago." He tried to sound casual, uninterested. The way Betts's eyes narrowed on him indicated he'd failed.

"She was in here with a man from back east. That's all I know about him." Pressing her lips together, Betts studied him a moment before saying what was on her mind. "Don't know why you stopped courting Frannie. Maybe I should've asked because you're a good man and she's real quality. Regardless your reasons, she deserves to be happy." Taking a couple steps, she glanced over her shoulder. "So do you, Zeke."

"It's so good to have you here, Aaron. Although, I am surprised to see you." Francesca took a seat across the desk from Edmund's best friend and business partner. Aaron Haas had always been kind to her, taken her defense when Edmund ended their engagement.

His brows drew together. "Didn't he explain my traveling to Splendor in his letters?"

She hesitated, trying to recall what her ex-fiancé had written. "I'm sorry, Aaron. He didn't mention your intent to come west. In fact, his letters were confusing."

Aaron glanced away, lips twisting in a scowl. "Do you still have them?"

"No. I read them before throwing them away."

Snorting out a chuckle, he squeezed the bridge of his nose. "I told Edmund not to write, that I should've been the one to contact you. Did he mention ending his engagement?"

"To the second unlucky woman?" Grimacing, she wished the words could be taken back. "Apologies, Aaron. That was quite inappropriate."

"But true." When he saw her eyes widen in surprise, he held up a hand. "Even though he's my business partner and best friend, his faults aren't lost on me. Edmund was a fool to end your engagement. He figured it out, but not before proposing marriage to another woman."

"Which he's now ended."

"True." Aaron leaned back, stretching out his legs to cross one ankle over the other. "He regrets breaking off your engagement."

"Would it surprise you that I don't care?"

Chuckling, he shook his head. "Not at all. In fact, I told Edmund as much."

This surprised her. "You did?"

"As bright as he is, Edmund can be a horse's ass."

Laughing, Francesca relaxed, ready to move away from a subject which held no appeal. "I believe it's time for you to explain your reason for coming to Splendor."

"I've always admired your habit of getting right to the point. Have you heard of the new copper mine near here?"

"Yes. Blue Bonnet Copper Mine."

"Correct. Did you know Edmund and I are the major shareholders?"

Jaw dropping, she gave a slow shake of her head. "How could that be possible? My understanding is an older man from Idaho discovered the copper and filed a claim. The locals have talked of nothing happening for over a year until recently, when new activity began."

"What you've heard is accurate. Except for the part about Edmund and I buying out the original claim owner. We own seventy percent. Two other investors own the remaining thirty. I've arrived to visit the site and hire a new manager."

"A *new* one?"

"The first died of a heart attack on his way to Boise to hire miners. We're in need of a replacement."

"Do you expect to find him here, in Splendor?" She couldn't hide the doubt in her voice.

"This is where I'll start. The mine is much closer to this town than going over or around the mountain range to Boise."

"I'd be happy to introduce you around. There are a number of people I believe will offer valuable information. Have you heard of Noah Brandt, Gabe Evans, or Dax and Luke Pelletier?"

"I understand the Evans family is from New York. Bankers and hoteliers, I believe."

"The same. Gabe is the sheriff and major shareholder of the Evans' hotels in New York. All three families are clients of mine. Chan Evans, his youngest brother, is a U.S. Marshal, and also owns shares in the family hotels."

"You're making my point for me, love. Splendor is a frontier town with big city experience. Even your banker, Horace Clausen, is from a large bank back east." Standing, he walked around the desk, taking her hand. "Are you ready to introduce me to the citizens of Splendor?"

Knowing she had no other appointments for the day, she took his hand, allowing her mouth to tip upward in a grin. "I am."

Zeke canvassed the businesses on Frontier Street, talking to everyone he could about Harmon Tibbs, and anyone they'd seen with a Bowie knife. What he learned about Tibbs didn't surprise him.

Not many people knew him. According to Horace Clausen, the bank president, Tibbs was a quiet man and hard worker. A widower with no children, he'd purchased the ranch east of town from the Bank of Splendor a few months before.

"I don't know who would've wanted him dead. He didn't have any enemies I know about. Except..." Horace rubbed fingers over his brow in a familiar, nervous gesture.

"Except what?' Zeke asked.

"A few months ago, I referred Tibbs to Miss O'Reilly to complete a will. He'd come into a small inheritance. You may want to speak with her about it. Plus, he withdrew a sizable amount yesterday."

"How much?"

"Three thousand dollars," Horace answered. "Did you find it on him?"

"No."

"I suppose he could've used the funds for something before he was murdered. Although, I couldn't imagine what he would've paid for with that much money."

Zeke didn't respond, tucking the information away before moving to his next question. "Do you remember anyone who carries a Bowie knife?"

"Well, we all know Cash Coulter does." Horace's gaze shifted to look out the window of his office toward the tellers. "I could ask my people. They meet almost everyone who lives in the area. Have you sent anyone to the ranch to speak with Harmon's hired men?"

"Gabe is sending one of the deputies out."

"Good. Maybe you'll learn more. In the meantime, I'll ask my people about anyone with a Bowie knife."

"I'd appreciate it, Horace."

Walking out, he stepped into the cool, early afternoon air. He'd already talked to the employees in the St. James and to Reverend Paige. His next stops were the Splendor Emporium and Finn's, one of two saloons not owned by Nick and Gabe.

The Emporium was owned by Josephine Lucero, the wife of a local rancher, and Olivia McCord, Doc McCord's wife. They offered finer products not available at the general store, and custom clothing designed by Allie Coulter, Cash's wife.

Not long after entering the store, he left without learning anything useful. His next stop was Finn's, the newest saloon in town. It offered a few more services than the Dixie or Wild Rose, meaning he'd be interviewing the women who worked upstairs.

"Afternoon, Finn." Zeke walked to the bar, waving off the bartender's offer of a drink.

"Deputy. What brings you in here this afternoon?" The middle-aged Irishman sipped a whiskey, assessing Zeke. "I heard about Harmon Tibbs. A good man. Don't know who would've wanted him dead."

He didn't mention the cash Harmon withdrew from the bank. "Do you know anyone who wears a Bowie knife?"

"Deputy Coulter."

"Anyone else, Finn?"

"You should talk to the gals upstairs. They see and hear a lot. Come with me."

Following Finn up the stairs, Zeke stopped outside the first door and knocked.

"Dahlia. Someone wants to talk to you." After a minute, Finn knocked again, louder this time.

Opening it a crack, the woman peaked out at him. "It's early, Finn."

"Harmon Tibbs has been murdered. Deputy Boudreaux has questions for you."

"Harmon?" Her voice trembled, the reaction not concealing the fact she knew the rancher.

"Last night, outside the Dixie. Do you know anyone carrying a Bowie knife?"

Opening the door a few more inches, Dahlia's gaze moved between the two men. "Bowie knife? Is that how Harmon was killed?"

"Yes," Zeke answered. "We're trying to find out which men wear a Bowie knife."

"I don't know for a fact, but I've heard Deputy Coulter has one."

"Anyone else?"

Staring at the wall across from her room, Dahlia's features seemed to freeze. "There was a man a few weeks ago. He carried a Bowie knife."

Zeke stepped closer. "Do you remember his name?"

Giving a slow shake of her head, Dahlia's face paled. "No."

"He didn't give you his first name?" Finn asked.

"No. It's not unusual for men not to give us their names. Or give us a false one. I suspect the man was married, and didn't want his wife finding out."

Zeke tamped down his growing eagerness. "Can you describe him?"

"It's been a while." Closing her eyes, Dahlia's mouth drew into a firm line. "He was older than me. Maybe thirty, but not much more. A little shorter than six feet tall, and slender. Dark beard and mustache. And his hair was a little longer than most. Dropped almost to his shoulders."

"Clothes?" Zeke asked.

"Nothing special. The same as any ranch hand would wear." Pursing her lips, she lifted her gaze to Zeke. "Except for the scar."

"What scar?"

"Started below his left ear. Trailed down his neck and across his chest to his stomach. I don't know how he lived through it. I'm guessing it was the reason he wore his hair so long...to hide it."

"Did you ask him about the scar?"

She shook her head. "Not my business."

"Has he been back?" Finn asked.

"No. But there's something else."

Zeke inched closer. "What, Dahlia?"

"I don't think he knew I saw it, but he had a brand. Right here." She pointed to her chest, just below the collarbone on her right side.

"Did you recognize the brand?"

She shook her head. "Sorry. Maybe I can draw it for you."

Thirty minutes later, Zeke left Finn's, Dahlia's drawing in his hand. He didn't recognize it, but knew someone who might.

The town was growing dark by the time he left Finn's. Hurrying down the street toward the livery where Noah Brandt might still be working his forge, he ducked between two buildings to cut the distance.

Ignoring his surroundings, focused on reaching his destination, Zeke didn't hear the footfalls behind him. Nor did he sense the lifting of an object until it slammed down on his head, plunging him into darkness.

Chapter Four

"We've done all we can today, Aaron. Would you join me for supper at Eagle's Nest?" Francesca walked next to him on Palace Street, her senses on edge in the increasing darkness.

"Supper with you is perfect, as long as you allow me to pay."

She'd expected his response. "All right. We can take a shortcut through here."

Walking between two buildings on their way to Frontier Street, a deep groan came from ahead of them. "Hello?" She walked faster.

Reaching out, Aaron grabbed her arm. "Frannie, wait. Let me go first." Moving ahead of her, they heard the sound again. "There."

He rushed to a crumbled body in the dirt, kneeling down. Touching the still form, he glanced up at Francesca. The man no longer groaned, nor did he move.

"Frannie. Go for help."

Rushing back the way they'd come, she hurried to the clinic, pounding on the locked door. Drawing it open, Doc McCord narrowed his eyes in question.

"A man's been injured. My friend is waiting with him."

"Let me get my bag and a lantern." A moment later, Clay returned, shutting the door behind him. "Show me."

"He's between the gunsmith and barber shops." Ignoring the stares of those they passed, Francesca stormed between the buildings. "Here, Doctor McCord. This is a friend of mine, Aaron Haas."

Handing her the lantern, Clay knelt next to the injured man. "Hold up the light, Frannie."

Lifting it to wash over him, she watched as Clay and Aaron rolled him onto his back. A gasp tore from her throat. "My God..."

"It's Zeke Boudreaux," Doc announced, ignoring her hand gripping his shoulder.

"Is he alive?" Her body trembled, intense pain squeezing her heart.

"Yes, but we need to get him to the clinic."

"Between us, we should be able to carry him, Doc." Aaron slid his arms under one side while Clay took the other. "One, two, three."

Lifting him, they moved toward the street. "Frannie, grab my bag."

She'd already picked it up, rushing behind them with the lantern. Reaching the clinic, Francesca moved ahead, opening the door. Another lantern already lit the interior enough to guide them toward the examination room.

"Frannie. Get Hex."

She didn't want to leave, not knowing if Zeke would be alive when she returned. Hesitating an instant, she sent up a quick prayer before running to Hex and Christina's house.

When the door drew open, Hex took in the panic on her face. "What happened?"

"It's Zeke. He's at the clinic."

Leaving the door open, he hurried to speak with Christina, grabbed his gunbelt and hat, and followed Francesca down the street. Entering, he spared a cursory glance at a man he didn't recognize before his boots pounded on the wood floor toward the exam room. Opening the door, the color drained from his face at the sight before him.

"Is he..."

"He's alive, Hex. Someone clubbed him pretty hard on the back of his head." Clay pointed to the large knot. "Francesca and Aaron heard him moaning, which is how they found him. All we can do now is wait."

"I'll sit with him, Doc."

Straightening, Clay continued to watch Zeke. "I suppose you'll stay around anyway."

"You're right." Grabbing a chair, Hex moved it next to the bed. "I'll be here as long as it takes."

Clay had stopped at McCall's before going home for a quick supper with his wife, Olivia, asking Betts to deliver meals for Francesca, Aaron, and Hex. He'd then made one more stop, surprised to find Gabe still at the jail.

"When did it happen?" Shoving out of his chair, he checked his gunbelt before picking up his hat.

"Sometime this afternoon. Francesca O'Reilly came to get me close to five. Hex is in the room with him. I'm going to have supper with Olivia, then return to the clinic."

"I need to let my deputies know what happened before checking on Zeke. I'll stay with Hex until you return."

"Whoever did this used a blunt object. A club or bat made of wood. The swelling is significant, Gabe." Clay let out a deep sigh. "I don't know yet if there'll be any permanent damage."

Having been a colonel in the Union Army during the war, Gabe had seen all types of injuries and too many deaths to count. He didn't intend to lose one of his deputies.

"Zeke is hardheaded, Doc. He'll come through this. We'll also find whoever attacked him."

Ignoring Aaron's urging, Francesca had refused to leave the clinic until Zeke woke up. She didn't intend to speak with him. Knowing he would recover was all she required before going home.

Although delicious, she picked at the food Betts had delivered, while Aaron cleaned his plate. Hex's remained untouched on a chair next to her. She couldn't imagine what he was feeling.

According to Christina, and from what she'd witnessed, Hex and Zeke were close. They'd traveled across country together, working with each other as deputies.

At one time, Francesca thought she might become part of the Boudreaux family. When Zeke backed away from their courtship without a word of explanation, she'd been devastated. Within a short period, two men she'd cared about had abandoned her. Zeke's rejection had hurt the most. Still did.

The sound of the door opening had her shifting toward it. "Gabe."

He walked to her, removing his hat. "Evening, Frannie. Have you heard anything?"

"Not yet. Hex is in there with him."

Gabe took in the man who'd stood when he'd entered. He extended his hand. "I'm Gabe Evans, the sheriff."

"Sheriff. I'm Aaron Haas, a friend of Francesca's family in New York. I've heard of the Evans family. Perhaps we can talk once your deputy has recovered."

"All right." Gabe returned his gaze to Francesca. "I'll be with Hex."

"Would you let me know if there's a change?"

Face softening, he nodded. "I will."

Taking the plate from her lap, Aaron set it aside. "How well do you know Boudreaux, Frannie?"

"Not well. I know Hex and his wife, Chrissy, better."

Reaching over, he covered her hand with his. "I believe that's the first time you've lied to me."

Her shocked expression met his before she looked away. "He courted me for a while before changing his mind. I've spoken little to him in several months."

"Changed his mind?"

"He stopped calling on me without explanation. There's nothing more I can tell you, Aaron."

"The man must be a complete fool, Frannie. Any man would be honored to have you for his wife."

She gave a disbelieving snort. "Men such as Edmund and Zeke?"

"They're both fools. I've said the same to Edmund." Aaron didn't mention it was one of the reasons he'd traveled such a long way to see her.

For years, he'd held a deep affection for Francesca, staying in the background, not voicing his feelings. His opportunity may finally have come, and Aaron hoped he had the courage to take it.

Standing when the door to the exam room opened, she steeled herself for what Gabe had to say. "Is he awake?"

A small smile curved Gabe's mouth. "Yes. He's in pain and disoriented, but awake. I'm going to find Doc McCord." Before he could reach the front door, it opened, Clay entering.

"He's awake," Gabe said before he could ask.

"Excellent." Walking past him, Clay joined Hex.

Francesca released a slow breath, relief coursing through her. Zeke would be fine. There was no reason to stay. She felt Aaron's hand on her elbow.

"Are you ready to leave?"

"Yes." She wanted to stay, see for herself Zeke would be all right. It hurt knowing he wouldn't want to see her. "If anything changes, Gabe, would you mind letting me know."

"Not at all. I'll send someone right away."

She lowered her head in an almost imperceptible nod. "Then we'll say goodnight."

Aaron slipped her arm through his. "A pleasure meeting you, Sheriff. I'll be in touch." Entering the street, he stopped. "Where do you live?"

"I'm two houses from the clinic. This way."

"Your own house?"

"Not exactly. I rent it from Noah and Abby Brandt. They built most of the houses in town. It's small, with one bedroom, but it suits me and isn't too far from my office."

"It seems you've made friends here."

She forced a smile, fighting the continued worry over Zeke. "Yes. It hasn't been hard. There are a great many wonderful people here. Many from back east. You'll meet many of them. I mean, assuming you'll be staying for a while."

"My plans are to stay for several weeks. Perhaps as long as a few months."

Reaching her house, Aaron walked in with her, lighting one of the lanterns. "This is quite nice, Frannie. I can understand why you selected it."

"There aren't many choices. One of the houses, or the boardinghouse. It would be too expensive to stay at the St. James for long. If you do decide to stay longer than a few weeks, you may want to speak with Noah. He has a small warehouse with furniture for those who need it. Gabe and Noah grew up together in New York."

"I should like to meet him."

"I'll introduce you tomorrow." She tried to suppress a yawn. "Sorry, Aaron."

"It's been a long day. I should be leaving for the hotel. Shall I come by in the morning to escort you to breakfast? After all, we weren't able to have supper at the Eagle's Nest."

She hoped his invitation would've caused more excitement. Instead, it reminded her of the many times Zeke had escorted her to breakfast when he'd still held an interest in her.

"Breakfast would be lovely. I'd be happy to meet you at the hotel. Their meals are excellent."

"Shall we say eight?" At her nod, he bent to brush a kiss across her cheek. "It's wonderful to see you, Frannie. I'm glad you're happy with the move west."

Closing the door behind him, she considered his words. She was pleased with her decision to leave the stifling life in New York behind. The trip by railway and stagecoach had been exciting, the town of Splendor a refreshing change from the crowds of a large city.

She cherished her friendship with Christina Boudreaux. With Rachel Pelletier over a half hour's ride from town, having a friend close provided a sense of security, as well as a way to lessen the loneliness of living and working alone.

Entering her bedroom, she changed into her sleeping gown, drawing the brush through her long, auburn hair. Staring in the mirror, Francesca found herself wondering what had made Zeke change his mind.

She'd never considered herself beautiful, but she was far from unattractive. No, it wasn't her appearance which caused Zeke to move on. Their time together had been comfortable, easy in a way she hadn't expected from a city girl and frontier lawman. They enjoyed each other's company, laughing, becoming friends.

Giving up, she set the brush aside, deciding torturing herself with *whys* would accomplish nothing. Zeke was out of her life, and he'd decided to keep the reasons to himself. Her acceptance offered no comfort.

She'd ask after him, confirm his recovery, then let it go. It was time to move on. Having Aaron in town would be a wonderful distraction. It would never turn to love, but they'd always have a solid friendship. For now, Francesca would content herself with what she could have, no longer grieving over what she couldn't.

Chapter Five

Beauty watched out the window of her upstairs room at the back of the Grand Palace. She'd been perched in this position for almost two hours, telling Ruby she didn't feel well enough to work.

Her location offered a clear view to the clinic across the street. She'd happened to be looking outside when Doc McCord and a man she didn't recognize carried Zeke Boudreaux inside, a woman with them. Her breath had caught at the sight of the handsome deputy, blood crusted in his hair. Since then, Beauty hadn't left the window for more than a few minutes, anxious to learn more.

Splendor had been a destination out of necessity, not desire. The long journey from Kansas City put distance between herself and a man she hoped to never see again. If she'd had more coin, Beauty would've traveled all the way to San Francisco. But her empty purse forced a shorter trip.

It had taken one day to obtain a position with Ruby as a waitress and dance girl. No one was forced to offer more to the male admirers, and so far, her wage and tips had sustained her enough to avoid inviting men to her room.

Back in Kansas City, she'd been the mistress of a rich, unmarried banker. Kyle Forshew had made it clear they'd never marry. After all, his reputation would crumble if he married a former prostitute.

Instead, he'd provided Beauty with an almost unlimited budget for whatever she wanted, an apartment, and access to a carriage and driver. *His dirty little secret* is how Beauty saw herself.

Although she had a few friends, decent women would cross the street to avoid her, their husbands looking the other way while taking sly, appreciative glances at her. At nineteen, and with no other prospects, Beauty had embraced the money and endured the nasty stares. And hoped Kyle would come to love her.

How wrong she'd been to pray for a life of respectability and acceptance. After three years, he'd settled her into the carriage for a picnic at the river.

Finishing their meal, Kyle had calmly informed her she had thirty days to vacate the apartment and leave Kansas City. Not because he'd met a woman he intended to marry. His intention was to replace her with another mistress. Younger and fresh in a way Beauty could no longer claim. At twenty-two, he considered her used up.

Kyle's words had cut deep. The dismissal humiliating. Tears streaming down her face, Beauty had run to the carriage, leaving the screaming, irate banker alone to find his own way back.

Reaching her apartment, she'd packed, intending to leave her now ex-lover behind. Stuffing all she could into two large satchels, Beauty retrieved the leather pouched filled with bills, and loaded everything into the carriage for the short trip to the train depot.

It wasn't until she'd reached Cheyenne, Wyoming, that she'd read the headline in a Denver newspaper a passenger had left behind.

Kansas City Banker Murdered. Missing Woman Suspected.

A knock on Beauty's door dragged her from the view of the clinic and her depressing thoughts. Leaving the window, she climbed into bed, pulling up the covers.

"Beauty. Are you awake?" The door pushed open, Ruby carrying a bowl of stew. "How are you feeling?"

"Better." It was a lie. Whenever she thought of her ex-lover, any optimism she held for a better future disappeared.

Setting the bowl next to the bed, Ruby looked her up and down. "Your eyes tell the truth, and you aren't better. What I don't know is if you're sick physically, or sick inside." She touched Beauty's forehead. "If you ever need to talk, I'm here."

Ruby walked to the window, staring down at the clinic. "I heard Zeke Boudreaux was beaten and left between the gunsmith and barber shops. He's at the clinic."

Beauty didn't admit she already knew. Nor would she give any indication of her attraction to the rugged lawman. Not even her ex-lover had stirred the desire burning for Zeke Boudreaux.

"Another man you can never have," she mumbled under her breath.

Turning from the window, Ruby's brows drew together. "Did you say something?"

"Only that I hope he's all right."

Ruby waved a hand in the air. "That young man is too darn ornery to die. I hope he saw who did it. I'd better get back downstairs. Never can tell what will happen down there. Now, you eat every bit of the stew."

The instant Ruby closed the door, Beauty returned to the window. It may be foolhardy and futile, but fantasizing about a respectable life with a decent man was the only dream she had left.

"You didn't see who hit you, Zeke?" Hex had spent most of the last two days by his brother's side. Even though he'd awoken after the severe blow to his head, Zeke had drifted in and out of consciousness.

"No." His raspy voice was broken from disuse. "I was on my way somewhere. Don't remember where." He closed his eyes a moment, making Hex believe he might fall asleep. "There was sudden pain, then...nothing until I woke up here in the clinic."

"Gabe said you were talking to townsfolk about Harmon Tibbs. Finn Hanrahan said you left with a drawing of a brand. Does that help?"

Letting out a shallow breath, Zeke tried to concentrate with the dull ache still pounding at the back of his head. "A brand?"

"Finn said one of the girls who works for him drew a brand she saw on one of her customers. You took it and left. Finn doesn't remember you saying where you were going."

"A brand," Zeke repeated for the second time.

"It must've had something to do with Harmon Tibbs."

"Tibbs?"

"The rancher killed with a Bowie knife," Hex answered, voice wavering. "Why don't you rest a spell, Zeke? We'll talk again later."

"Sure, Hex."

A sharp pain hit his heart. Doc McCord warned Hex there could be some damage to Zeke's brain. Short or long-term. They wouldn't know for days, weeks, or even months. The knowledge didn't ease the ball of rage burning in his gut at whoever attacked his younger brother.

Placing a hand on Zeke's arm, he squeezed lightly. Hex had sent up prayers for him to live. Now the prayers were to have him back, the way he was before taking a shortcut between two buildings, gripping the drawing of a brand. A drawing he didn't have when Francesca and Aaron found him. Hex had to figure out who Zeke was in such a hurry to see.

Finn swore no one except him and Dahlia were present when she gave him the drawing. Hex couldn't shake the sense someone knew what Zeke had, attacked him, and took the image of the brand. Hadn't they realized Dahlia could provide another one?

Besides the drawing, nothing had been taken. Zeke's gun, money, and badge were still on him when Aaron and Clay had carried him to the clinic. All of this pointed to a brand being the reason someone almost killed Hex's brother.

"How's our patient?" Clay bent over the bed, checking Zeke's pulse, breathing, and eyes before straightening. "Have you spoken with him this morning?"

"A little. His memory isn't too good. Doesn't remember the man who was murdered or the drawing of a brand."

"Doesn't mean a lot right now, Hex. Later today, tomorrow maybe, he could recall everything. It was a vicious blow to his head. Many men would've died from it." Clay placed a hand on Hex's shoulder. "Give it some time. I've got a sick boy in the other room who needs tending. Come get me the next time Zeke wakes up."

Hex sat still as stone, watching the rise and fall of his brother's chest. He thought of them growing up, pulling pranks as young boys do, running through the streets of New Orleans without thought to the hard choices they'd be making as men.

The war came and both volunteered for the Confederate Army, served together, came home to a failing business and father broken in heart and spirit. It had been tough times, but they'd weathered it together.

When Zeke stirred, mumbling in an incoherent voice as the covers fell away, Hex reached out, pulling them back over him. Sitting back, he leaned forward to rest his arms on his thighs, staring at the floor.

He didn't know how much time passed between Zeke stirring and a soft knock on the door. Before he could respond, Francesca stepped into the room.

"Doctor McCord said you were in here, Hex. I hope it's all right for me to come by."

Standing, he ran a hand through his hair. "It's fine, Frannie." The weariness in his eyes and voice wasn't lost on her.

"I'd be happy to sit with Zeke while you take a break." Francesca looked behind Hex to settle on the still form. "How is he doing?"

"He's woken up a couple times. Doesn't remember much, but Doc says it'll take time."

Nodding, she moved closer to the bed, her breath catching at the deathly pallor to Zeke's skin. His hair was matted with sweat, dirt, and streaks of dried blood.

"If you're certain, I could use a few minutes to talk with Gabe. Maybe he's learned something."

"I don't mind at all, Hex. Take all the time you need." She watched him struggle, deciding whether or not to leave his brother. "I'll find you if he wakes up."

Nodding, he settled the hat on his head, taking one more look at Zeke before leaving the room.

Alone, Francesca let out a ragged sigh when her gaze traveled back to the injured man on the bed. She'd never said the words, but her feelings for Zeke had grown intense while he'd been courting her. So much deeper than what she'd ever felt for Edmund.

When he'd stopped calling on her, she'd felt a great tearing in her heart. Seeing him struggling for his life and a return of his memory, she experienced the pain all over again. He no longer wanted her, found her desirable, but his desires didn't matter at this moment. All she could feel was a feverish need to locate Zeke's attacker and bring them to justice.

Francesca had never handled a criminal case, didn't have the training or desire. For the man who'd become so important to her, she'd become whatever was required to bring him justice. If that meant becoming the best prosecutor in Montana, she'd do it.

Placing her reticule on a table, she sat down, scooting the chair closer to the bed. Somewhere in her readings, Francesca recalled human touch helped patients to recover. It was a wild and unsubstantiated notion, but she'd do anything to help.

Opening her hand, she reached out, settling her fingers around his bare arm. She didn't squeeze, waiting to see if her touch had any effect. A moment later, Zeke stirred.

Anticipation shot through her when his lips parted. When his head swiveled toward her, Francesca almost released her grip. Staying quiet, she watched as his eyes opened, blinking to focus on her.

"Frannie?" Her name rasped from his lips.

A small smile brightened her face, warm eyes meeting his. "I'm here, Zeke."

Closing his eyes, he opened them again. "You're much better looking than Hex."

Chuckling, she swiped at a tear before he could spot it. "I should get Doc McCord and find Hex." She began to rise when he shifted toward her.

"Wait. Tell me what happened."

Instead, she picked up a glass of water, holding it to his lips while supporting his head with her other hand. "Drink a little, then I'll tell you what I can." She held it close as he took a few small sips. When finished, she carefully let his head rest back on the pillow.

Wincing, he lifted a hand, feeling the lump on his head. "Someone hit me."

"Yes."

"I left Finn's with a drawing of..." He closed his eyes, opening them seconds later. "Dahlia drew a brand she'd seen on one of her customers."

Anticipation soared at his words. "Yes."

"Noah. I wanted Noah to look at it."

Eyes wide, the reason became clear. "Because he makes the brands."

Chapter Six

Doc McCord, Hex, and Gabe gathered around the bed, Francesca staying back to allow them room. When she'd intended to leave, Zeke lifted his head from the pillow, insisting she stay. His request didn't make sense, given how he'd avoided her for several months. Staying would cost her nothing except time, and she'd spare that for Zeke.

Clay laid a gentle hand on his shoulder, pushing him back down. "You aren't going home until I'm satisfied you can be there alone."

"He can stay with Chrissy and me."

"Other than the pain knifing through my skull, I'm fine. Besides, you have two young girls at home, Hex."

Crossing his arms, Zeke's older brother glared down at him. "We can make it work. The girls can sleep in the living room and you'll have their bed."

"Lena and I have two extra bedrooms," Gabe offered.

"Plus your father, son, and baby Emma." Closing his eyes a moment, Zeke tried to shake his head, wincing at the pain. "I appreciate the offer, Gabe, but home is where I want to be."

Clay ended that kind of thinking. "Then you need someone to stay with you, or at least make meals and check on you several times a day. I'm not allowing you to leave the clinic unless you take Hex's or Gabe's offer, or find someone to stay with you."

Tiring, Zeke's features showed his frustration. "How will you stop me?"

"Easy." Gabe pulled a pair of handcuffs from his back pocket, holding them up.

"I should've thought of those," Clay said.

"If you won't stay with us, Chrissy and I can take turns coming by several times a day, bring you meals."

"You have a job and Chrissy has obligations with the girls."

"You're being obstinate," Hex growled.

"I'm not an invalid. I'll find someone to make my meals."

"I can do it." Francesca's words were soft, almost missed by the three men. Hex was the first to turn toward her.

"What did you say?"

"I'd be happy to stop by with meals. That is, if Zeke is all right with it."

The men stepped away from the bed. Zeke's features made it obvious he thought it a terrible idea. Moving to the door, she rested her hand on the knob.

"Never mind. I'm sure you'd rather have someone else. Well...I should go." Before she could open the door, Zeke pushed up on one arm.

"Wait, Frannie." Slipping back onto the bed, he cleared his throat. "Are you certain you have time?"

"I have to cook for myself, so making enough for two isn't hard. It would be easiest for me to fix breakfast for both of us, but I'd bring lunch and supper." She looked at Clay. "Is there anything else I should know?"

An amused grin tipped the corners of the doctor's mouth. "Let me know if you notice a change. I'm keeping him here until tomorrow afternoon. By then, he should be able to take care of other...*needs*...on his own."

"All right. I'll come by the clinic in the afternoon." Her gaze moved between the men. "Gentlemen."

Waiting until she'd left, Hex turned toward his brother, unable to hide a smirk. "She's a real fine woman, Zeke."

Jaw tight, he closed his eyes. "Yes."

"You may have to find a way to explain why you acted like a horse's ass."

Gabe and Clay hid their smiles.

"She's bringing meals, Hex. Nothing more." Letting out an uneven breath, he opened his eyes to slits. "There's no longer a need to explain anything."

The three married men shot each other a knowing look.

Gabe headed to the door, settling his hat down, shading the bleak look in his eyes. "Good luck, Zeke. I'm thinking you're going to need it."

Francesca sat at her desk, head in her hands, wondering what had inspired her to offer Zeke help. Deciding it must have been a momentary lack of sanity, she dropped her hands on a groan.

She couldn't get out of it now. Telling herself it included nothing more than providing meals for a few days made her feel a little better.

Staring at the papers before her, Francesca tried to focus on work. Aaron would be spending the next two days at the copper mine, giving her a great deal of time to think. About her life, Zeke, and Aaron.

She hadn't missed the interest in her friend's eyes. Aaron had always tried to hide how he felt about her, having no desire to come between her and his best friend, Edmund. If only she'd fallen in love with him instead of the man who'd so callously humiliated her.

Uncaring of society's standards, Aaron had grown up the son of a middle-class accountant, who'd passed along his belief in loyalty and hard work. Francesca had never been clear on how he and Edmund had met. To most people, they didn't appear to be suitable. Except for one critical factor. Compared to Edmund, Aaron was brilliant.

He could smell an excellent business proposition, work through the details in his head, and guide the venture to success. Edmund made the introductions, Aaron evaluated and finalized the deals. One had the money, the other the skill. And somehow, they'd become friends.

Now Aaron had traveled to Splendor to visit one of their investments. From Edmund's two letters, she knew it had to be somewhat new. Certainly after she'd left New York. Which made her wonder why they'd taken on a business so far from home.

Scanning the contract for a new mine manager, Francesca found the words dancing before her. She'd promised Aaron to have it ready when he returned. When he rode out of Splendor, his intention had been to speak with the miners, discover if one had the experience he sought. She didn't believe he'd find his man without a more thorough search.

A rap on the door gave her a welcome respite from staring at the paper before her. Shoving from the chair, she opened the door, eyes landing on a woman she'd heard of but never met.

"Miss O'Reilly. I'm Nellie Crawford. I wonder if you'd have time to speak with me."

"Of course. Please, come in and have a seat." Opening the door wide, she motioned to the chairs in front of the desk.

Sitting down across from the young woman, Francesca folded her hands together. "I hope I'm not being rude, but are you the woman people call Beauty?"

Eyes widening for a mere moment, Nellie raised her chin. "It's a name I'm not fond of, but yes, it's what most people call me."

"Well, Miss Crawford, tell me how I can help you."

Opening her reticule, Nellie removed several folded pieces of paper. "I am asking you to keep this safe for me." She slid it across the desk.

With a wary expression, Francesca unfolded the papers and began reading, not once looking up. Finishing, she lifted her gaze to Nellie's.

"Do you have any proof of the charges in this letter?"

"That is what I *believe* happened and who was involved, Miss O'Reilly."

Francesca refolded the letter, setting the papers down before her. "So you have nothing to substantiate the accusations. What are your intentions?"

Nellie's haunted silver eyes turned a deep gray as they narrowed on Francesca. "To find proof of the treachery and clear my name."

"By yourself?"

Gripping her reticule, Nellie's lips drew into a taut line. "I still have a few friends in Kansas City, plus I do have some money available to hire help."

"A private detective such as a Pinkerton agent?" Francesca glanced down at the paper before returning her attention to Nellie.

"Perhaps. I'd hoped to obtain your guidance on this matter."

"Do you realize what you're asking, Miss Crawford? If you've been accused of murder as your letter states, and if it's discovered I'm assisting you, I could lose everything. Sheriff Evans might even arrest me."

"Miss O'Reilly, there is no one else I can approach. To be certain, there is a risk to you. However, I'm asking just two things. First, keep the letter safe. Second, provide advice on what I should do next." Reaching into her purse, she withdrew money. "This is to retain your services. Let me know if it is not enough."

"The money is not the issue. It's the nature of the business. You cannot go to Sheriff Evans or his deputies for help. Do you know if there's a wanted poster on you?"

"I've never seen one."

Francesca's brows drew together. "Could it be you've never been charged with the crime? The letter mentions an article in the newspaper. Have you obtained any confirmation?"

"I've been too afraid to ask."

"All right. I'll agree to keep the letter for you. I have ways to learn if you have been accused of killing Kyle Forshew, and if wanted posters have been issued. That's all I'll agree to at this time. You will say nothing about our association. Do you understand?"

A relieved sigh escaped past Nellie's lips. "Yes. Thank you, Miss O'Reilly. When should I expect to hear from you?"

"You're living at Ruby's, correct?"

Nellie gave a slow nod.

"I'll get a message to you. Can you leave without anyone seeing you?"

A small smile tipped the corners of Nellie's mouth. "The same way I came. You're back door is mere steps away from Ruby's." Pulling the hood of her cloak over her head, she met Francesca's wary gaze. "Thank you."

With that, she hurried out the door and down the back steps.

Fluffing the pillow behind Zeke's head, Christina grabbed the blanket to pull over his chest.

"I'm not an invalid," he groused with a slight grin. Zeke was glad to be out of the clinic and home.

He planned to be out of bed and back to his duties as a deputy within two days, half the time the doctor instructed. His gaze moved to the wall clock next to his wardrobe. Almost four o'clock. Unless she changed her mind, Francesca would be arriving soon with his supper.

"What more can I do for you, Zeke?" Christina set a pitcher of water and glass by the bed. Hex stood next to her, his arm around her waist.

"You've done more than enough, Chrissy. Take Hex home and have supper with your family." He regretted the words, seeing Hex stiffen and Chrissy's stricken face.

Wincing, she moved closer to the bed. "You *are* our family, Zeke." A soft knock on the door broke the growing tension.

"I'll get it." Hex opened the front door to find Francesca with a basket over her arm, holding a pot. "Hello, Frannie. Let me help you." Taking the pot from her hand, he stepped aside, following her to the kitchen.

Setting the basket filled with biscuits on the table, she looked past Hex to the bedroom. "How is Zeke doing?"

"Ornery, but good. He wants no part of staying in bed."

"Can you blame him?" She slid from her shawl, laying it across a chair.

Chuckling, Hex gave a sharp shake of his head. "No. I'd be as irritable as him. Come on."

Hesitating in the doorway of his bedroom, Francesca took a moment to study the man in the bed. Zeke appeared tired, but relaxed, a man pleased to be home.

Walking to the end of the bed, she waited for him to notice her. When their eyes locked, he tried to sit up, groaning at the pain in his head.

"Stay down, Zeke." Francesca moved to the opposite side of the bed from Christina. "You won't recover if you keep fighting common sense."

"I believe it's time for us to go home, Chrissy." Hex tugged at her arm. "I'll be back tomorrow, Zeke. Thank you for bringing his supper, Frannie."

Waiting until the door closed, she turned back to Zeke. "How's your head?"

"Fine," he ground out, the edge to his voice saying the opposite.

Reaching out, she gripped the blanket, pulling it up to cover his chest. "Are you hungry?" When her hand lingered a moment, Zeke rested his over hers.

"Why did you offer to help me?"

Francesca's throat thickened, not having a good answer. "I honestly don't know."

Chapter Seven

Redemption's Edge Ranch

"Where's Billy?" Dax Pelletier calmed his chestnut stallion, Hannibal, waiting for the last of the group riding to the Blackfoot village. It had been too long since they'd visited Chief Running Bear and his grandson, Swift Bear.

Bull Mason, Travis Dixon, Tat Whalen, Sam Rinehart, and Billy Zales would be riding out with Dax. The last two, Sam and Billy, along with three other orphans, had been made a part of the family after the five were found years before hiding in a damp cave. Sam and Billy had come a long way, growing into impressive young men.

The sound of pounding hooves had the men looking toward the southern pasture. Billy reined up next to them.

"Sorry, Dax. I found a stray calf by the river. She wasn't too inclined to leave."

"Thanks for retrieving her, Billy. All right, men. Let's get going. I want to reach the Blackfoot camp by early afternoon."

Except for Sam, all the men had been to Chief Running Bear's village. A few years earlier, the people at Redemption's Edge ranch had saved his grandson's life. Swift Bear wouldn't have lived without the medical treatment provided by Dax's wife, Rachel, and her uncle, Doc Worthington.

Dax and his brother, Luke, made sure to visit the village at least twice a year, each time taking a couple steers. Today would be no different. They'd cull a couple from the herd in one of the northern pastures. In exchange, Running Bear would offer deer skin moccasins, pipes, necklaces, and hairpieces for the women.

There were times the chief insisted they spend the night. Dax didn't know what to expect from this visit. Rare were the days with little to do around the ranch, and with six men riding to the village, he planned for a short visit before riding back.

A mile from the camp, Bull spotted the familiar sight of Blackfoot braves following them on the ridge across from their trail. Shifting in his saddle, he grinned, seeing several braves a quarter mile behind them. He'd expected them, would've been concerned if the riders hadn't been guarding their village.

A hundred yards out, women left their tipis, children huddled in small groups, and the older men watched their approach through eyes wise from many years of dealing with enemy tribes and other whites.

The braves Running Bear kept in camp held bows, arrows at the ready. A few carried rifles, their backs straight, gazes locked on the white men. The Pelletier men didn't flinch, nor did they rest their hands on the six-shooters at their sides, or rifles in scabbards.

About ten yards from the first tipi, Dax held up his hand, stopping them. From experience, he knew Chief Running Bear would emerge from his lodge or the trees when he was ready. It could be two minutes or two hours. Dax and his men would wait atop their horses until he appeared.

Over a year had passed since Billy rode with Dax and a few others to the Blackfoot village. Not much had changed. The location close to Wildfire Creek was where he remembered. His count of tipis and horses had remained about the same.

The reason he'd asked Dax to be included today had nothing to do with tipis or horses. His gaze wandered over the village, searching for one person. A beautiful, young Blackfoot woman with a smile he'd never been able to forget.

While Dax, Bull, and Running Bear had disappeared into the chief's tipi, Billy had taken a walk by the creek, picking wild berries and popping them into his mouth. When he'd gone as far as intended and turned around, a vision stepped from among the bushes.

Long, black hair had been braided, draping over one shoulder. Her round, dark brown eyes were wide with curiosity as she studied him. When he'd taken a step closer, she'd moved away. They'd continued with him moving forward and her stepping away for a long time, the entire time communicating with hand signals and her broken English.

Her name was Shining Star, younger sister to Swift Bear, and granddaughter to Chief Running Bear. Billy had guessed her to be about seventeen, but she'd only smiled when he'd asked her age.

They'd walked for several minutes before someone from the village called her name and she ran off.

"Do you see her?" Bull's deep voice cut into his thoughts. He was the only other person who knew about his walk with Shining Star.

Billy shook his head. "It's been a year. She's probably married with a child by now."

As he finished, the flaps of one tipi flew open. Running Bear stepped outside, head high, back straight, he walked to within a few feet of Dax.

"Dax Pelletier. It is good to see you." His gaze moved to Bull. "Bull Mason. You are welcome. Come. We will talk."

Dismounting, Bull slid off his large roan gelding, Abe, handing the reins to Billy. "Talk to the people. Maybe Shining Star will join you." Briefly clasping Billy's shoulder, he followed Running Bear and Dax into the chief's tipi.

"This is my first time here. Let's walk around." Sam stood beside him, eyes wide as he took in the village.

"Sure. Just don't touch anything. Be careful what you say. Some of them speak English."

Leaving the horses with Travis and Tat, they took their time walking through the village. An elder sat in front of his tipi, sharpening a knife. Finishing, he looked at them, features impassive.

"May I see it?" Billy asked, pointing to the knife.

Without a word, the elder handed it to Billy. Running his thumb along the edge, he grinned, handing it to Sam. He did the same, testing the sharp edge, nodding at Billy before giving it back to the elder.

As they moved on, a group of children ran beside them. They spoke among themselves, laughing, pointing to the gunbelts around each man's waist. Reaching the far end of the village, they made a slow turn.

Billy hadn't seen Shining Star, or her brother, Swift Bear. He didn't know how he felt about not being able to talk to her again.

Glancing around, his gaze caught on a group of riders in the distance. He didn't move, waiting as they got closer. Sam stood next to Billy, not breaching the silence.

A chorus of whoops accompanied the group's arrival. Billy recognized Swift Bear, but not the other braves. The last to arrive was a brave about his age. Beside him rode Shining Star.

Her face showed no recognition. She glanced at him, sliding off her horse, but not closing the distance between them. Quite the opposite. She moved closer to the brave, not meeting his gaze.

"Billy Zales." Swift Bear took the few steps to stand before him. "It is good to see you."

"It is good to see you, too, Swift Bear." He introduced Sam, not allowing himself to look at Shining Star. "Your English has gotten better, my friend."

"Grandfather says those who can see the future know we must learn to speak the white man's language. There is a woman at the fort who teaches us."

Fort Connall was located a few hours north of the Blackfoot village. The Pelletiers and Gabe Evans had helped forge a relationship between Running Bear and Colonel Miles McArthur.

As they spoke, Shining Star and the brave walked past, her gaze averted. It was clear the two held a deep fondness for each other. The knowledge didn't bother him. Shining Star had been a beautiful distraction, someone to think about during the long nights bedding down with the herd.

"Did you come alone?" Swift Bear asked as they retraced their steps to where their horses waited.

"Dax Pelletier and Bull Mason brought us," Billy answered.

Spotting the two steers up ahead, Swift Bear stopped. "My grandfather will make a trade for them."

Billy gave a slow nod. It wasn't his exchange to make. As they walked past Running Bear's tipi, the flap opened, the men exiting.

"Billy, Sam. Running Bear has invited us to stay tonight. There will be a feast in our honor." Dax didn't give away how he felt about the delay in returning to the ranch. He'd already made his preference known on the ride north.

Sam's wary gaze latched onto Billy's, unable to hide his concern at staying in the Blackfoot village. Years before, Sam and his two sisters had been Crow captives for one year, Billy and his sister for three. They'd been treated as slaves, beaten for no reason, and starved. Knowing the Blackfoot were nothing like the Crow didn't ease their apprehension.

"We'll be all right, Sam. Dax wouldn't have accepted if he believed we'd be in danger."

"You're right, Billy. Unlike before, we're men, able to protect ourselves."

After a short conversation with his grandfather, Swift Bear joined them. "Come. I will show you where you will sleep."

Billy huddled into his bedroll inside the tipi they'd been provided. The chorus of snores indicated the other men were asleep. All except Dax. He'd chosen a spot outside the entrance of the tipi. Rolling over, Billy wished he'd done the same.

The minutes crept by, his mind refusing to close down enough for sleep. He didn't think about Shining Star. His thoughts were on the Crow, wondering where the renegade band camped. It wouldn't be unusual for them to place their village within striking distance of other tribes.

The Crow had found a loose peace with the whites, learning English, some becoming scouts for the Army. The problem was a violent group of anti-whites who'd broken off from the main tribe a few years earlier. They were the band who'd held him and the other orphans captive.

Billy knew the leaders had changed since he'd been held hostage. He'd heard from trappers and pioneers heading west the band was still ruthless, hatred ruling them.

They raided farms, ranches, and other tribes to get what they needed. Food, horses, captives. The Blackfoot had been their target often. After finishing a meal of venison, beef, rabbit, and fish from the nearby stream, he'd asked Swift Bear how long it had been since the Crow had attacked. The brave had stayed silent a long moment before shaking his head.

Rolling to his other side, Billy huffed out a frustrated breath. He knew it had to be past midnight. Dax had announced they'd be rising before sunup to get an early start on the trip home. With six of them gone for two days, there'd be a good deal of work waiting for them at the ranch.

Billy didn't know how much time passed before his body gave up and he drifted off. His dreams consisted of long ago images of his feet being tied to a stake, water and food placed inches beyond his reach. Even in sleep, he could feel the pangs of hunger, the twisting of his gut.

Stirring, his eyes popped open. He lay still, relaxing when he heard nothing for several minutes. Burrowing deeper into his bedroll, Billy closed his eyes. Drifting off a second time, an odd sound from outside had him sitting up.

Glancing across the tipi, his gaze met Bull's. Both sat still, listening. Something spooked the horses, their alarmed whinnying waking the other men. Spearing feet into their boots, they grabbed their rifles and six-shooters. Bull was the first one out.

Dax was already up, holding his rifle when shouts and blood-curdling cries came from the trees surrounding the camp. Without further warning, the crack of rifle fire rang through the camp, hitting the dirt around them.

Billy lifted his rifle. "It's the Crow. We're under attack."

Chapter Eight

Dax crouched, rifle tucked against his shoulder, firing one shot after another at the Crow rushing through the village. The war cries of their attackers were almost as terrifying as the bullets from their guns.

The Blackfoot warriors scrambled to defend their families while the Pelletier men dropped to the ground, making themselves smaller targets as they squeezed off their own shots. Screams of pain and anger could be heard over the continuing rifle fire.

A sharpshooter during the Civil War, Bull aimed and shot over and over, dropping one Crow warrior after another. Dax and Travis did the same while Tate, Billy, and Sam did their best without the experience of the other three.

The attack ended within minutes, the Crow retreating, taking several Blackfoot horses with them. The assault didn't last long. Still, the ground was littered with bodies from both tribes. Young men and old.

Billy rose, stunned at the ferocity of the surprise attack. Surveying the carnage, his gaze landed on a young woman cradling the body of a warrior in her lap. Rocking back and forth, a keening sound blew through her lips. It was then he recognized her and the person she held.

Running toward her, Billy dropped to his knees. Reaching out, he tried to check for life before her small hands brushed his attempts aside.

"Shining Star?"

Her damp, agonized eyes met his, a slow shake of her head saying what her words wouldn't. The young brave was dead. *Her* young brave.

Dax and his men stayed until they'd helped move the bodies. The women did most of the work, preparing the dead for the journey before them. Shining Star worked beside her brave's family, tears streaming down her face. The sight broke Billy's heart. She'd never be his, but he hated seeing such a sweet girl in pain.

After completing all they could, the men saddled their horses for the trip back to the ranch. Running Bear thanked them, providing provisions for the ride, pouches of sweet grass and sage, and strands of beads for the women. None were necessary, but Dax and Bull knew the chief would not accept the cattle without giving something in return.

Billy took a minute to approach Shining Star, who sat alone behind her family's tipi, keening as her body rocked back and forth. He stood over her a moment before crouching down.

"I'm sorry, Shining Star." Billy knew she heard and understood, even as her eyes remained closed, tears glistening her cheeks.

Standing, he hesitated a moment before turning away, leaving her to her grief.

Splendor

Francesca picked at the meatloaf she'd ordered for lunch at the boardinghouse, her thoughts on Zeke. This morning at breakfast, Doc McCord had given him approval to return to work.

For two days, she'd prepared and eaten each meal with him. She'd kept her distance, answering his questions about her work and happenings in town, but not offering more.

"Did Zeke go back to work today?" Georgina Wise, a nurse who'd traveled with Francesca and the other women to Splendor, slid a bite of meatloaf into her mouth. Doctors McCord and Worthington had just hired her and another nurse, Carrie Galloway, to work at the clinic.

"He couldn't get out of bed and dressed fast enough."

"Did he explain why he stopped calling on you?" Carrie asked. Shy and unassuming, she had no interest in finding a husband.

Looking away, Francesca shook her head. "It doesn't matter. He lost interest, maybe met someone else."

"Or he's simple minded." Georgina stabbed her fork in the air. "What else could explain how any man would walk away from you?" She whirled her fork before scooping up a bite of potatoes.

Surprised by her friend's antics, Francesca couldn't hide the first smile she'd had in a while. "I'm sure he had his reasons."

Carrie shook her head. "Georgie's right, Frannie. The man may be a good lawman, but that doesn't mean he isn't a fool." Picking up her cup of tea, she held it to her lips. "As my father would've said, a true eejit." This brought chuckles from the other two women.

"Uh-oh. I believe your friend from back east has arrived." Georgina tilted her head toward the front door. "Aaron?"

Glancing behind her, Francesca forced a grin when he walked toward them. After spending the last two days making meals for Zeke, she wanted to spend time alone or with the women at this table.

"Frannie." He bent down, brushing a light kiss across her cheek. "Ladies." He'd met Georgina and Carrie briefly when he'd first arrived in town. "May I join you?"

"Please," Georgina answered. "How was your trip to the Blue Bonnet?"

Thanking the server for bringing him a cup of coffee, he glanced at Francesca before turning his attention to the other women. "The copper mine is quite impressive. I may have found a man with enough experience to become the new manager."

"That's wonderful." Francesca put as much enthusiasm as possible into those two words.

He didn't notice the flat tone of her voice. "I'm giving him a couple weeks to see how he handles the men."

"Does that mean you'll be staying for a while?" Georgina set down her cup, face flushing. If Francesca wasn't mistaken, her friend had developed an interest in Aaron. It would be so much easier if he found a real love interest. Unlike her, a woman who could commit to him.

"It appears I'll be staying several weeks. I'm going to speak with Noah Brandt about renting one of his houses. Perhaps the empty one between Frannie and the clinic. She mentioned he has a storage shed with extra furniture."

Carrie leaned toward him. "She's right. I've been through it several times. There's enough to furnish at least four of his houses."

Francesca listened to the conversation between the three without contributing. Her thoughts remained on Zeke. He'd had many chances to explain his reasons for ending the courtship, but chose to stay silent. As much as his silence hurt, it gave her the answer she'd sought for months.

She simply hadn't meant that much to him.

"We should visit the Splendor Emporium. I heard Mrs. Paige is working for Josie and Olivia."

Georgina's comment drew Francesca's attention. "The reverend's wife?"

"The same. Josie told me she's in the shop a few hours a week. The three of them are having a wonderful time, and Mrs. Paige is proving to be an excellent saleslady." Georgina opened her reticule, pulling out some money.

"I'll be paying, ladies. May I escort you to the Emporium?" Standing, Aaron assisted Carrie and Georgina from their chairs, moving around the table to Francesca.

"I'm staying for a while, Aaron." She had plans, but didn't want to share with him.

"Alone?"

A soft chuckle burst from her lips. "I've been alone for quite a while. I'll be fine."

"Allow me to escort you to supper tonight, Frannie."

"I'd enjoy that, Aaron."

Seeing a smile brighten his face, she relaxed. He'd been her friend through difficult times, understood her reasons for moving to Splendor, and traveled thousands of miles to visit, even if the official reason was to check on the copper mine.

"Would six o'clock suit you?"

"Fine."

Squeezing her shoulders, Aaron joined Carrie and Georgina at the front door.

Watching the door close behind them, Francesca checked the time on her pendant. Her guest was late.

Fidgeting with the edges of her napkin, her gaze wandered over the other customers in the large dining room. No one paid her any attention.

When she'd received the note requesting a meeting late this morning at the boardinghouse restaurant, Francesca had almost refused. It wouldn't be wise to be seen together, but something stopped her. The wording in the note, perhaps the tone of the message. Whatever it was, she'd sent a reply, agreeing to the meeting.

Her body startled when Beauty took a seat next to her. She hadn't seen or heard the woman approach. She'd dressed in a demure day dress with long sleeves and high collar, a hat, which shielded much of her face, and gloves.

"Hello, Miss O'Reilly. Thank you for agreeing to meet with me."

"Miss Crawford. Your note made it sound urgent."

Licking her lips, she kept her gaze focused on her lap. Opening her reticule, Beauty pulled out a telegram, handing it to Francesca. "Please, read it."

"May I bring you something to drink?" Rose Keenan, a school teacher by training and one of the women who'd traveled west with Francesca, worked for Suzanne Barnett as a server. Outgoing with an easy nature, she had more than one man interested in courting her.

"Tea would be wonderful," Beauty answered.

"I'd like the same, Rose." Francesca had an urge to introduce the women, deciding it would be best to keep Beauty's identity private for now.

Smiling, Rose whirled around, stopping at another table before disappearing into the kitchen.

Remembering the telegram, Francesca unfolded it, reading it twice. "It's not signed. Do you know who sent it?"

"I believe it came from Louis Elder."

Francesca recalled Beauty's letter, the one in her office safe. "He's the man who implicated you in Kyle Forshew's death."

They waited while Rose set down cups of tea before each of them. "Would you like to order anything else?" Both declined, staying silent until they were alone again.

Studying the telegram again, Francesca's lips pursed. "If you're right, Louis Elder is clearly threatening you. How did he find you in Splendor?"

"I don't know. I've contacted no one since leaving Kansas City. The truth is, after Kyle broke off our association, nobody would've cared if I left. At least that's what I believed until seeing the story about Kyle being murdered."

"And you being implicated."

Beauty's features stilled. "Yes."

"I know this isn't what you want to hear, but we should speak with Sheriff Evans."

"No."

Francesca understood. "I do have some good news."

Lifting her face, Beauty's eyes showed a small amount of hope. "What is it?"

"There's a deputy in Big Pine who owes me a favor. He agreed to go through the wanted posters."

"What did he find?"

A small smile appeared on Francesca's face. "Nothing."

"No wanted posters on me?"

Shaking her head, Francesca reached out, touching Beauty's hand. "Not that he could find."

"What does that mean?"

Pulling back, she lifted the telegram. "Now we concentrate on finding who wants you dead."

Chapter Nine

Zeke leaned against the outside wall of the telegraph office, arms crossed, hat settled low on his forehead, watching the two women talk inside the boardinghouse. He'd been stunned to see Beauty, wearing a simple cotton dress, cross the street to join Francesca.

Numerous questions raced through his mind. How did they meet? What would they have in common to talk about? Why would Francesca choose to meet Beauty in such a public place? If it was business, why not meet in her office or at Ruby's? He'd get answers...just not now.

An hour passed before Beauty left, walking down the boardwalk toward the St. James Hotel, not once looking in Zeke's direction. Several minutes later, Francesca stepped outside, glancing around. He knew the instant she spotted him.

Her gaze flicked away from his before she took another cautious glance at him. They stared at each other a long moment, neither moving.

Zeke cursed himself for not talking with her during their meals together. He'd wanted to, but the words never came. Francesca never asked. In fact, their brief conversations stayed far away from the time he'd courted her.

The lawyer in her asked questions about the night he'd been attacked. She'd been patient at his lack of recall, encouraging him to tell her even small details. He couldn't. The minutes right before and after the assault were a blank.

Making a quick decision, his gaze still locked on Francesca's, he stepped into the street, avoiding riders and wagons on his way to meet her. Waiting for a large Conestoga carrying a family to pass, he continued toward her.

Zeke half expected her to be gone. Instead, Francesca stood in the same spot, hands clasped in front of her. His heart banged against his ribs, his steps slowing. Touching the brim of his hat, he offered a small smile.

"Hello, Frannie."

"Deputy Boudreaux."

He hadn't expected such a formal, or icy, greeting. "I never had a chance to thank you for bringing meals to me."

"It wasn't a problem. If you'll excuse me, I must return to my office." When she started to turn away, he stepped closer.

"Frannie, wait."

She ignored the discomfort in his voice. Francesca had no desire to have a conversation with him on the town's boardwalk or anywhere else. He'd had plenty of time to talk with her during the hours she'd sat in his bedroom eating one meal after another. Impatient, she met his gaze.

Removing his hat, Zeke fingered the brim. "Do you have time to talk?"

Cocking her head, she lifted a brow. "About?"

Glancing away, he swallowed, struggling with how to respond. "I wanted to explain."

"If you're talking about the way you ended our courtship, there's no need. Now, if you don't mind..." She took a step away before he reached out to touch her arm.

"You deserve an explanation."

Her chest squeezed, throat constricting. For so long, Francesca had hoped for him to explain what caused him to stop calling on her. He'd chosen to keep his reasons to himself. After almost four months, she was still curious, but no longer cared.

Straightening, chin lifted, her green eyes blazed at him. "I deserved to hear your reasons months ago. They no longer matter to me."

She'd gotten several feet away before he called after her. "Why were you meeting with Beauty?"

Stopping, she turned back to him, keeping the anger to herself. "She's a client. The reasons are confidential. Good day, Deputy Boudreaux."

Zeke wanted to go after her. Instead, he stayed in place, refusing to follow. He'd seen the pain in her eyes, her rigid stance. Talking to Francesca now would serve no purpose.

Watching her retreat down the boardwalk, he winced when spotting Aaron Haas walking toward her. A moment later, she'd slipped her arm through his, never once looking back.

Shoving the hat down on his head, he stared after them. Regret coursed through him for being such a fool by not realizing all he had with Francesca. Giving a quick shake of his head, he reminded himself he did know.

Instead of talking, explaining how she deserved more than a lawman with no real home, little savings, and few prospects for a better life, he'd stopped calling on her. Almost dying from the blow to his head, he'd had a great deal of time to think about his future, the mistakes of his past. Without doubt, Francesca was his biggest.

"Ride out with me to the copper mine. It's a beautiful day, and I believe you'll enjoy seeing what the men are doing." Aaron followed Francesca into her office, setting his hat on a table. "We can discuss the contracts on our way."

She'd planned to study the documents Beauty had given her, making her own notes on the people and places. "I don't have the time, Aaron. There are clients I can't put off any longer." She reached for a stack of papers, pulling out a single sheet. "This is the contract for a mine manager you asked me to prepare."

Taking it from her hand, Aaron sat down, placing it on his lap. "We'll make it a short trip, Frannie."

She shook her head. "I'm sorry, but not today. Another time, when I'm not so busy." Francesca looked up at the knock on the door.

"Are you expecting someone?" Aaron asked.

"No." Walking around the desk, she pulled the door open. For a moment, she could only stare. Then a shriek of pure joy burst from her lips. "Nancy!"

The best friends engulfed each other in an excited hug before dropping their arms. "I can't believe you're here. Why didn't you tell me you were coming?" Francesca grabbed her friend's hand, tugging her into the office.

"I wanted to surprise you." Nancy looked past her to the man standing. "Aaron?"

"Hello, Nancy." He moved forward, kissing her cheek.

"My father told me you'd left New York for business, but I had no idea you'd come west."

"Edmund and I are the majority owners of Blue Bonnet Copper Mine. It's in the mountains near Splendor. I'm here to check on our investment."

"This is such a wonderful surprise, Nancy. How long can you stay?" Francesca couldn't contain her excitement.

"Until you send me back home." There was a joking tone in Nancy's voice, as well as something more. "Is there a chance you have room for me until I find suitable lodgings?"

"You'll stay with me as long as you want. Did you just arrive?"

"On the one o'clock stage, and I'm starving."

Chuckling, Aaron headed to the door. "I'm going to leave you two ladies alone to catch up and eat. Nancy, please join Frannie and me for supper tonight."

"I'd love to, Aaron."

"Excellent. See you at six o'clock."

When the door closed, Francesca took a considering look at Nancy, noting the pinched lines around her eyes and mouth. "When did you last eat?"

Shrugging, she absently brushed dust from the skirt of her dress. "Yesterday. I wasn't hungry this morning."

"Where is your luggage?"

"Mr. Griggs at the stage station let me leave it inside his office until I learned where to take it. There isn't much. Mother gave me money to buy what I needed."

Francesca's brows drew together, deciding to wait and ask her questions while Nancy ate. "Let's get you some food. McCall's is right next door."

Stepping outside into the bright afternoon sun, Francesca and Nancy walked the few steps to McCall's. There were several tables empty at this time in the afternoon.

"Anywhere you want, ladies." Betts walked to where they sat down, focusing on the woman she'd never seen before. "I'm Betts Jones. I own this place with my husband, Elmer."

"It's a pleasure, Betts. I'm Nancy Rucker, a friend of Frannie's from New York."

"We've known each other since we were children," Frannie added.

"Well, I hope you'll be visiting us for a long time. Maybe you'll like Splendor enough to stay. I'll bring coffee while you decide what you want."

"We'll both have your meatloaf and potatoes, Betts."

Nodding, the older woman left for the kitchen.

Waiting until Betts couldn't hear, Frannie leaned toward Nancy. "All right. It's time for you to tell me why you're here."

Nancy's face heated as she struggled to look surprised. "Do I need a reason besides missing my closest friend?"

"I've known you a long time. You don't do anything without a good reason."

Shoulders slumping, Nancy's face fell as she leaned back in her chair. "You're right, Frannie." A small amount of relief flowed through her when Betts brought their food. "Do you mind if I eat a little before explaining?"

Francesca picked up a fork, pointing it at her. "Not at all. But don't even think I'll forget about getting an explanation."

Nodding, Nancy dug into her food. They ate in silence for several minutes before she set down her fork.

"My mother has asked my father for a divorce."

Francesca's eyes opened wide, brows arching. "What? Your parents have one of the best marriages I've ever seen."

"We all thought so." Nancy looked out the window, her face pale.

"Did your mother say why?"

Giving a slow nod, Nancy let out a strangled sigh. "She discovered Father's been keeping a mistress. I don't know for how long. It's a woman he met at a social function. A widow about ten years younger than Mother." Sad eyes met Frannie's. "We all know it's not uncommon for men of our social status to keep a mistress, but Mother always trusted Father. It broke her, Frannie. I've never seen her so distraught."

"She decided divorce was the only answer?"

"The only way out of an intolerable situation. She'll wait until the divorce is final, then join me out here."

"What did your father say?"

Snorting, Nancy shook her head. "He ended his relationship with the mistress and begged Mother for another chance. He swears it won't happen again. Told her he still loves her. Has always loved her..." She glanced away, swiping at a lone tear escaping down her cheek. "My brother is in his last year at West Point. He won't even speak to Father. You know how devoted he is to our mother."

Offering a slow nod, Francesca set her napkin on the table, her appetite gone. "She won't give him another chance?"

"Mother doesn't believe she'll ever be able to trust him again. She thinks he's only concerned about what people will say and the financial effect to him. He'll lose a great deal of his wealth to Mother."

"Which is only fair."

"I agree. Still, watching their pain is hard. Mother sent me here so I won't have to face my friends."

Reaching over, Francesca placed her hand over Nancy's. "I'm so glad she did. This is where you belong."

They both looked up at the sound of the front door bell ringing. Drawing in a surprised breath, Francesca removed her hand from over Nancy's.

Zeke walked inside, nodded at Betts, then came straight to their table. Removing his hat, he motioned to the empty chair. "Do you mind if I join you?"

Nancy spoke before Francesca could decline. "That would be wonderful, Deputy."

"Nancy, this is Deputy Zeke Boudreaux. Zeke, this is my closest friend, Nancy Rucker. She'll be staying with me for a while."

"My pleasure, Miss Rucker." Reaching into his pocket, he pulled out a telegraph. "Bernie Griggs gave me this. He told me you asked for directions to Frannie's office. I was on my way to deliver it, but saw you in here." He held out the message to Nancy.

Opening it, she gasped, her eyes rolling back an instant before Zeke caught her from slumping to the floor. Standing, Frannie rushed around the table, grabbing the telegram, reading it.

"Oh, no." She placed a hand over her mouth.

Holding Nancy in his arms, he watched Frannie. "What is it?"

"Her father is dead."

Chapter Ten

"How are you feeling, Miss Rucker?" Clay McCord bent over the bed in the clinic, checking her eyes.

"Fine. A little humiliated at fainting."

"Don't be. You had some terrible news."

The impact of the telegram's contents slammed into her again. Her father was dead. "Yes, it was." Leveraging herself up on one arm, she let out a tired sigh. "May I leave now?"

"Let me assist you." Placing a hand behind her back, he supported Nancy as she sat up, then slid to the ground. "Frannie and Zeke are out front." Opening the door, he walked next to her as she joined them.

"Nancy." Francesca went straight to her, as did Zeke. "How are you?"

"Fine. Sorry for all the trouble I've caused."

"You've been no trouble. Anyone would've responded the same," Francesca said.

"I need to send a telegram to Mother. The message didn't say how he died." Nancy tried to hold back a sob. "She doesn't want me to come home."

"There must be a reason," Francesca said. "Would you like me to send a telegram to her?"

Zeke put a hand on the small of her back. "Why don't you take Nancy home? I'll send the telegram. Bernie will make certain the answer gets to me."

"Thank you, Zeke." Nancy walked on leaden feet to the door, Francesca and Zeke beside her.

"We'll be at the house. I appreciate you doing this." Francesca touched his arm, quickly pulling her hand away.

"I'll be over as soon as I get a reply."

He headed toward the telegraph office while Francesca looped Nancy's arm through hers for the short walk to the house.

She stopped in front of a whitewashed home with steps to a small porch. "This is mine."

Gaze moving over the small structure, a small smile curved Nancy's lips. "It's adorable."

Laughter burst from Francesca's lips. "I thought the same when Noah showed it to me. Let's go inside and I'll fix you some tea."

"Sounds perfect."

While Francesca heated water, Nancy took a minute to look around before joining her in the kitchen. "It's wonderful, Frannie."

"It's tiny."

"But it's yours. Does your friend, Noah, have others?"

Francesca turned from the stove. "You're welcome to stay here as long as you want."

Sitting in one of two wood chairs at the small kitchen table, Nancy's features fell. "Mother said I shouldn't come home. There must be a reason she wants me to stay out here. I'm hoping her response to Zeke's telegram will explain why." Grasping her hands together, she rocked slightly. "If I don't return to New York for a while, I'll need a place of my own. Or a room at a boardinghouse. There is one in Splendor, isn't there?"

Fixing tea for them, she set the cups on the table, taking the other chair. "A very nice one. Suzanne Barnett owns it, along with her husband, Nick, and his business partner, Sheriff Gabe Evans. They also own the St. James Hotel, along with the sheriff's wife, Lena. The problem is the boardinghouse is often full."

Staring into her cup, Nancy couldn't help the tears pooling in her eyes. "I can't believe he's dead."

"Had he been ill?"

"No. In fact, he hadn't been sick in years. Then Mother learned about the other woman."

The bitterness in her friend's voice broke Francesca's heart. Mr. and Mrs. Rucker always appeared to be so much in love. He doted on his wife, daughter, and son. His actions didn't make sense. Francesca thought of Edmund, and how it had been easy for him to break their engagement in favor of another woman.

"I know this sounds awful since he's already dead, but I hate what he did to our family." Taking a sip of tea, Nancy again swiped at the moisture on her face. "Did I tell you they'd planned a trip to Europe in a few months? Before Mother discovered his cheating."

"No."

"Father refused to cancel it. Why would he encourage the trip if he loved another woman?"

Swallowing the lump of pain building in her throat, Francesca shook her head. "I don't know."

"And now we may never know."

"You've been gone several weeks, Nancy. Who knows what happened between your parents during that time. He may have explained everything. Your mother may have forgiven him."

Jumping up, Nancy paced to the front window, looking toward the houses across the street. "And unicorns do exist." Raising both hands to her face, her body shook on a deep sob.

Wrapping her arms around her closest friend, Francesca's own tears streaked down her face. They stayed this way for several minutes, until Nancy stopped shaking, the tears subsiding. Dropping her arms, Francesca stepped away at the sharp rapping on the door.

Zeke stood on the front porch, a telegram in his hand. "May I come inside?"

She shot a quick glance at Nancy before pulling the door wide. "Please. Would you like tea or coffee?"

"Nothing, thank you." He took cautious steps toward Nancy. "I received a reply."

Red rimmed eyes met his. On a sigh of resignation, she held out her hand. "Have you read it, Zeke?"

"No, and Bernie doesn't share private correspondence." He glanced at Francesca, motioning toward the kitchen. "We'll give you a minute alone to read it."

The kitchen didn't give them much privacy, but it would have to do. Taking another telegram from his pocket, he lowered his voice.

"You know Walter Evans is in New York."

"Gabe's father?"

"Yes. Gabe sent him a telegram asking for anything he knew about Mr. Rucker's death. A reply came back right after Nancy's mother sent her latest telegram." He moved so Nancy couldn't see him handing Francesca the message from Walter Evans.

Reading it, she glanced up, her face pale, features drawn. "This is horrible. Do you think Nancy's mother included the same in her reply?"

Zeke shook his head. "I don't know, but I wanted you to read what Walter sent."

"Frannie?" Nancy's trembling voice had them turning to face her, the telegram dangling from her fingers. "Papa was murdered."

Nancy and Francesca had begged off going to the Eagle's Nest for supper with Aaron. Zeke offered to bring food from McCall's, allowing the four of them to talk in private about what happened to Nancy's father.

Picking at her food, Nancy looked up. The tears were gone, but not the emotional anguish of losing her father. The message from her mother had been brief, saying he'd been murdered and the police were searching for his killer. The telegram from Walter Evans had contained much more detail. Francesca had been the one to make the difficult decision to let Nancy read that message.

"Why didn't Mother tell me the police are looking for his mistress? And why tell me to stay out here instead of going home?"

"To protect you," Aaron answered.

Nancy's brows drew together. "From what?"

"It's more about protecting you from *who*." Zeke set down his fork. "The mistress didn't accept your father ending their relationship. The police are looking for her, but from what I know of New York, there are thousands of places to hide, and people who might be willing to help her."

"But she's a murderer," Nancy rasped out, angry and in obvious pain.

Zeke offered a slow nod. "Possibly. People make decisions that seem strange to the rest of us. Your mother may believe returning to New York could put you in danger. It would be best to stay here until they find the woman."

"What would you do if you went home, Nancy?" Aaron stretched out his legs, crossing them at the ankles.

"Help Mother with arranging the services, pack Father's clothes, go through his papers." Shrugging, she tossed her napkin on the table. "Although my brother will be there to help her."

Frannie placed a hand over Nancy's. "You'll be safe here. There's so much I want to show you."

"I've been trying to convince Frannie to ride out to the copper mine with me. Why don't you come with us on Saturday, Nancy?"

"If that's what Frannie wants, then I'd love to ride out. Anything to get my mind off what happened."

Zeke looked between the three, feeling as if he were invisible. Shoving up from the table, he moved toward the door. "I need to get to the jail. You know how to find me if you need anything."

Francesca joined him, stepping onto the porch, leaving the door open. "Thank you for your help, and for bringing supper, Zeke."

His gaze flashed to Aaron, who was talking with Nancy. "Is he courting you, Frannie?"

"What?"

"Aaron. Is he courting you?"

"Not that it's your business, but no, he isn't."

Zeke looked down at her, snorting. "He wants to."

Frannie showed no surprise at his comment. "Maybe. It's not the reason he traveled to Splendor. Aaron's here to check on his investment in the Blue Bonnet Copper Mine. He and his business partner own the majority interest."

Zeke knew a little about Edmund, but not all of it. "Are you interested in him?"

Francesca glanced behind her to see Nancy and Aaron still talking. She felt no spark at the sight of him, nothing to compare to her feelings for Zeke. As much as she'd hoped to forget him, it had never happened.

"He's been a friend for years."

Zeke tilted his head. "That's not what I asked, Frannie."

Crossing her arms, she fought to control her rising anger at a question undeserving of an answer. He'd been the one to end their courtship, making it clear he had no further interest in her. What did he care if Aaron wanted more than friendship?

"I know what you're asking, Zeke." Looking up at the stars, she let out a shaky breath, making a rash decision. "There was a man a few months ago who I cared a great deal about. I believed he felt the same. It was a humiliating experience to realize how wrong I was."

"Frannie..."

"What I'm attempting to say is, given my history with men, I no longer allow myself to have expectations."

"Frannie..."

Ignoring the misery in his voice, she lifted a hand, placing her palm on his chest. "Someday, you'll find a woman who'll capture your interest. Someone you want more than any other. That woman obviously isn't me." Turning, she stepped through the doorway and into the house. "Goodnight, Zeke."

Chapter Eleven

Wes Acker rode through the thick brush to his camp several miles northeast of Splendor, his gaze scanning ahead and behind him. Feeling the familiar itch, he reached up, absently scratching the scar on his chest. The brand had healed years ago, yet there were days it felt as fresh as when the men had held him down, burning it into his skin. He'd made certain none of them lived to see their next birthday.

Reaching his camp, Wes rode the perimeter, thankful to find nothing had been disturbed. He'd made the long ride to the territorial capital of Big Pine, staying for a few days before returning.

Dismounting, he removed the saddle, tack, and saddlebag before building a small fire. When he'd made his last, brief visit to the Wild Rose, he'd heard rumors of the sheriff and his deputies searching for a man with a scar on his face and carrying a Bowie knife. Wes had quickly tucked his away, keeping his hat low to hide his scar. Instead of the two whiskeys he'd intended, Wes settled for one before riding hard for Big Pine. It had given him time to consider his next move.

There wasn't much he could do about the scar. The new Bowie knife had been stashed in his saddlebag, and wouldn't come out until he'd crossed the border into Wyoming, Idaho, or the Dakotas.

Reaching into his saddlebag, Wes pulled out a strip of jerky, tearing off a bite with his teeth. Turning around, he walked toward a large bush several yards away. Dropping to his knees, he began to dig. A moment later, his hands touched a leather pouch containing three thousand dollars. A sneer crossed his face. That money would take him a long way to wherever he wanted to go. He should've taken it with him to Big Pine and ridden out from there. But he hadn't, forcing him to return to his original camp.

Returning to the saddlebags, he stuffed the pouch inside, lowering himself onto a long-dead log. Staring at the flames while chewing the dried meat, he thought about his past and uncertain future.

Becoming a hired gun had come easy to him. He'd always had a fast hand and steady eye, hitting targets before others had drawn their six-shooters. While his friends learned how to run cattle or train horses, he'd practiced a completely different set of skills.

At nineteen, he'd left his family's ranch. Ten years later, Wes was still riding, sending money home, but never feeling the desire to return.

Tearing off another piece of jerky, he stilled at the sound of approaching horses. Jumping up, he kicked dirt on the fire, continuing to cover it until he'd doused the flames and eliminated the smoke.

His heart raced as the pounding hooves came closer. Tacking up and mounting, he reined his horse in the opposite direction. Wes had made it less than twenty yards when an arrow whizzed past his head.

Reaching down, he struggled to draw his gun while guiding his horse between trees and thick brush. Spotting a group of boulders up ahead, he leaned as low as possible over his horse's neck before reining behind the large collection of rocks.

Sliding off, he slapped his horse before firing wildly with his gun as he drew his rifle from the scabbard. Thrusting the six-shooter into his holster, Wes dropped to a knee. Placing the butt of the rifle against his shoulder, he waited one...two...three seconds, pulling the trigger when the first rider reached him.

Tumbling backward over his horse, the Indian was dead before hitting the ground. Firing again, another man flew off the back of his horse, his head crashing into a tree.

Hearing nothing, Wes hunkered down and waited. He counted five minutes, then ten, but didn't move from his position behind the boulders. The horses belonging to the riders he killed didn't return. He continued to listen for any type of movement, the sounds associated with a threat. The wind whipped through the trees, making it difficult to be certain if he was alone.

Wes estimated at least an hour elapsed before he convinced himself the danger had ended. Shoving up to stand, he groaned at the pain in his joints and back. At twenty-nine, he felt old and used up.

He'd considered quitting the life of a hired gun many times, discarding the idea each time. Wes hated ranching, and knew nothing else. Over the years, he'd met other guns for hire who worked for one person, generally a rich rancher who'd achieved his wealth by driving out smaller spreads. It worked well for both. The fast gun had steady employment and a powerful man to deflect the law. In return, the rancher had a man he could depend on to do his bidding.

Whistling, he relaxed when his horse appeared in the darkness. Mounting, Wes spared the bodies of what he recognized as Crow warriors a short glance, feeling no guilt at leaving them before deciding to ride out. Everything he owned was already stowed in his saddlebags, including the money in the pouch, and what he already had sewn into the edges of his bedroll.

Shifting in the saddle, he took a quick look around, listening, hearing nothing. Making a quick decision, he kicked his horse.

Francesca closed the journal on her desk, ready to meet Aaron and Nancy downstairs. She'd agreed to make the trip to the mine to meet the manager who still had another week to prove himself. It would be good to be away from town a few hours, clear her head and enjoy the company of friends.

She hadn't seen Zeke since leaving her house after supper a couple nights earlier. Francesca didn't know what had possessed her to share a little of how his backing away a few months ago had hurt her. Admitting how his defection had changed her desire for a relationship with any man had surprised her even more. Those were private thoughts she'd shared with no one else.

She hoped being so open with Zeke would stop any further questions about Aaron, or worthless excuses about his actions months earlier. Nancy's visit had helped her focus on what was important. Friendships and work.

Francesca had done little to build her law practice, relying on work and referrals from the Pelletiers, Brandts, and Gabe Evans. They and their friends had kept her busy to the point she worked late many nights and the occasional Saturday. The schedule had kept her mind off Zeke while increasing the size of her savings account.

Reaching the front door, she stepped into a beautiful, early fall day. Suddenly, the idea of a ride to the mine excited her. Waiting on the boardwalk, she waved at the approaching wagon. Aaron held the lines, Nancy beside him.

"Isn't it a glorious day, Frannie?" Nancy asked when Aaron jumped down to help her onto the wagon seat. It was good to see a smile on Nancy's face. The first since hearing of her father's death.

"It certainly is." Francesca sat next to her, glancing behind her to see a basket in the back of the wagon.

"I ordered food from Suzanne." Aaron lifted the lines, stopping at a shout from behind him. "He made it."

"Who?" Francesca shifted to look behind them, breath hitching at the sight of Zeke riding up.

"Good morning, everyone." He tipped his hat at the ladies. "Thank you for the invitation, Aaron."

"Glad to have you along." Slapping the lines, Aaron grinned at him. "You're a much better shot than I am."

"Expecting trouble?" Francesca asked, brows scrunching together.

Zeke reined next to her side of the wagon. "You've been here long enough to always expect trouble, Frannie. Do you have your gun?"

She knew he was right. Outlaws, renegade Crow, wild animals, and other threats required travelers to be vigilant. A few months ago, there'd been a murder in Suzanne's boardinghouse restaurant. Soon afterward, Francesca had begun carrying a five-shot pocket revolver in her reticule at Zeke's urging. Something positive she took away from her brief relationship with him.

Nancy's eyes widened, mouth gaping. "You have a gun, Frannie?"

"Yes. We should talk about you purchasing one. Zeke taught me how to use mine."

"But..." She caught her bottom lip between her teeth.

"This isn't New York City, Nancy. We're in the middle of the frontier. There are dangers you can't imagine."

"She's right," Zeke added. "I can help you pick out a gun and teach you how to use it."

Nancy shook her head. "I don't think so."

"You should consider it," Aaron said. "I've been told most women out here know how to shoot."

Nancy's mouth pinched into a frown, unconvinced. "Do you have a gun, Aaron?"

Leaning down, he picked up a rifle from under the seat. Setting it down, he pulled back his jacket to expose a holstered six-shooter. "Since you're planning to stay a while, I believe you should accept Zeke's offer to help you."

They rode in silence for quite a while before Aaron turned onto a narrower trail toward the mine. A sign had been erected showing two miles to Blue Bonnet Copper Mine. He took another turn, the trail heading uphill before leveling out.

"Not much longer, ladies. The mine is about thirty minutes away." Aaron worked the lines, guiding them through the deep ruts.

He watched Zeke ride ahead of the wagon, hand on the butt of his six-shooter, his gaze constantly moving. It had been a smart decision to invite the deputy to ride with them.

During his last trip to the mine, Aaron had heard about a band of renegade Crow attacking travelers and ranchers, even attacking the Blackfoot village north of Redemption's Edge ranch. From what they'd told him, years ago, the same band had kidnapped some of the young men and women now living at the Pelletier ranch. So far, the Crow had left the mine alone.

The trail straightened at the top of the hill, Nancy's reaction instantaneous. "Oh, my. I've never seen anything so beautiful."

Zeke slowed to ride alongside the wagon. "Thunder Valley is spectacular. There are two waterfalls you'll be able to see once we get closer." He spoke to all of them, even as his attention didn't waver from Francesca. "There's a spot up ahead perfect for us to have lunch."

"Sounds perfect. Isn't that right, Frannie?"

Unable to tear her gaze from Zeke's, she offered a crisp nod. "Yes, Nancy. It does sound perfect."

Aaron watched the two, surprised at their obvious attraction. For the first time, he wondered if there might be more to the friendship between Francesca and the deputy.

"It does sound perfect, Nancy." Guiding the wagon around a tight turn, Aaron glanced at Zeke. "We'll visit the mine, then I'd ask you to show us the best place to eat our lunch."

Zeke forced himself to switch his attention from Francesca to Aaron. "I know an excellent spot. We'll be able to see both waterfalls."

"Excellent." Aaron increased the pace when the trail evened out, the ruts not as deep the closer they got to the mine. Taking the last turn, the mining camp opened up before them.

Nancy straightened on the wagon bench, rising a few inches to get a better view. "This is incredible, Aaron. I don't see any mine shafts. The men are working outside."

"It's called open pit mining." The words had scarcely left his mouth when an explosion shook the area, scaring their horses.

Pulling back on the lines, Aaron gained control with the help of Zeke while the women clutched the edge of the seat. Another explosion spooked the horses a second time.

Zeke abandoned his attempt to calm the horses. Dismounting, he rushed to the side of the wagon, gripping Francesca's waist, swinging her to the ground before doing the same with Nancy.

"Stay back," he warned the women. Climbing onto the seat, Zeke took the lines from a flustered Aaron, expertly calming the horses. "Take the women to the mine office. I'll drive the wagon."

Aaron jumped to the ground, motioning for Francesca and Nancy to join him. Taking the short path to the office, he opened his mouth to explain the purpose of the explosions when a third blast of dynamite had them covering their heads. A minute passed before they felt it safe to look back toward the office.

Gasping in surprise, Francesca ran forward, getting a better view through the whirling dirt and smoke. The office was gone.

Chapter Twelve

No one moved for several seconds, stunned at the sight before them. Zeke settled the horses for a third time, jumping off the wagon to join them. He turned toward Aaron.

"Keep the women here while I check to see if anyone was injured." When Francesca moved to join him, Zeke blocked her path. "We don't know if there are more explosives. Wait here with Aaron and Nancy." Turning away, he rushed toward what, a minute before, had been a small structure built of wood and stone.

Francesca stared after him, wrestling with the decision to follow or stay behind. Zeke reached the destroyed building at the same time several miners arrived at the site. No one spoke as they searched for signs of life.

"Was anyone inside?" Zeke asked the group of men, seeing nothing to indicate the office had been occupied.

A burly man with a thick beard and short hair stepped forward. "We don't believe so. The manager rode to town early this morning and hasn't returned."

Taking a few steps away, he placed fisted hands on his waist. "How could this happen?"

Shaking his head, the man grabbed a handkerchief from a pocket, wiping his brow. "Someone had to set it."

Zeke showed no surprise, his gaze raking over the remains. "Have there been problems?"

Scratching his beard, the man's mouth twisted into a rueful smirk. "A few of the men weren't happy with the choice for the new manager. Don't think they'd destroy the office because of it."

Eyeing the man, Zeke cast him a cautious look. "Are you one of the men who didn't agree with Aaron's choice?"

"Not me. He doesn't have much experience, but I've got no problem with him. He can read and write, which is better than a good number of us. Besides, most of the men already know what we're doing." He walked away, joining the other miners.

"Find anything?" Aaron stood beside him, Francesca and Nancy a few feet away.

"Nothing. It appears the office wasn't occupied. One of the miners said the manager rode to town early this morning and hasn't returned. This wasn't an accident. Someone set the charge, destroying the office. It's a miracle no one was inside. Have you heard of problems since hiring the new manager?"

Aaron picked up a ruined piece of wood siding, tossing it into the smoldering pile of rubble. "No. I hired him for a period of two weeks to see how he performed. It's been one week. Until this, work has been progressing well."

Zeke shoved his hat back on his head. "We should talk to the other miners. One of them may have seen something."

Aaron glanced behind him at Francesca and Nancy. "I'll let the women know to stay by the wagon."

Zeke shook his head. "No. We'll keep them with us." Shifting around, he approached the women. "We need to talk to the miners and I want you with us." He grasped Francesca's arm, gently tugging her along, with Nancy following.

"Did you, uh…find anything?"

Zeke knew what she asked. "No one was inside, Frannie. We want to talk to a few of the men, and I don't want to leave you and Nancy alone."

Pursing her lips, her attention hooked on something behind him. "We can take a tour while you're speaking with the men. Surely one of the minors would show us around."

"There's not much more to see than what's in front of you. If you want a tour, we'll do it after Aaron and I are finished."

Francesca's eyes flickered with irritation. Since arriving in Splendor, she'd become used to making her own decisions, not allowing men to order her about. The one time she'd allowed it was when Zeke had courted her. It had been an immense mistake.

Crossing her arms, she blew out a frustrated breath. "If that's what you want."

Knowing he'd think her petulant, she stomped away. At the moment, she didn't care. Francesca had grown tired of him showing up after months of nothing. No explanation or excuses, inserting himself back into her life.

She didn't want him there. Right now, she didn't want to be anywhere near him. As soon as they returned to town, Francesca would let him know.

Splendor

Francesca locked the front door while Nancy lit oil lamps in the living room and kitchen. It had been a long day, ending with a brief supper at McCall's she hadn't wanted to attend. She'd tried begging off, but Nancy reminded her it was supper with the men or eating at home, where they'd have to cook for themselves.

She and Zeke had spoken little since their tense discussion at the mine. After talking with several miners, Aaron had explained basic copper mining operations, giving the women a brief tour before helping them back onto the wagon.

The picnic and ride back to town had been uneventful. Aaron and Nancy spoke to each other most of the way. Zeke had ridden ahead of the wagon while Francesca busied herself with thoughts of the work waiting at the office.

She'd been thinking about hiring a secretary to help with the increased amount of work. The number of clients had tripled, and with the continual increase in those settling around Splendor, she estimated the need for another lawyer within a year.

Joining Nancy in the bedroom, Francesca changed into her sleeping gown, brushing her long, auburn tresses until they shone. "You and Aaron seem to be getting along quite well."

"I don't know why it would surprise you. We may not have spent much time together before arriving in Splendor, but we've been friends for years. Unlike many men our age at home, Aaron is easy to talk with, not arrogant or..."

"Haughty," Francesca suggested.

"Or conceited," Nancy corrected. "I enjoy his company."

"It appears he enjoys yours, also. Perhaps when you return to New York, he'll ask to court you."

Nancy leaned against the dressing table where Francesca sat. "It's doubtful since I don't know if I'll be going back."

Shifting on the small bench to look at Nancy, a grin tipped the corners of her mouth. "Truly?"

"Mother insists I stay for now, and honestly, I very much like it here. I've never seen such extraordinary country. It's so different from the crowds of the city. Do you mind introducing me to Mr. Brandt? I want to speak with him about renting one of his houses."

"Of course not. I believe the one next door has one bedroom."

"That would be wonderful, Frannie." Nancy moved away from the dressing table, lowering herself to the edge of the bed. "Tell me about you and Zeke."

The brush slipped through her fingers to land on the dressing table. She twisted to look at Nancy. "Zeke?"

"There's something between the two of you and I want details." Settling herself against the headboard, she dragged a blanket over her legs. "Please don't tell me there's nothing, Frannie."

Walking to the window, her gaze swept over the star-studded sky. "There isn't anything between us." The unmistakable sadness in her friend's voice told Nancy a great deal.

"Was there?"

Continuing to stare at the sky, Francesca gave a slow nod. "A few months ago. It didn't end well."

Straightening against the headboard, Nancy's eyes grew wide. "Do you want to talk about it?"

Turning away from the window, Francesca slumped into a chair. "There isn't much to say. Zeke courted me for a short period of time. It ended a few months ago." Rubbing her temple, she let out a sigh. "He never explained why."

Slipping off the bed, she sat on a settee near Francesca, tucking her legs under her. "What happened?"

"Nothing. He simply stopped calling on me." Her distressed gaze met Nancy's. "Zeke never had the nerve to tell me his reasons."

"The scoundrel. I wouldn't have assumed him to be such a reprobate. Why, I'd like to hunt him down and slap him until his head rattles."

Francesca threw back her head, laughing at Nancy's intensity.

"I'm serious. What kind of man would court a woman, then walk away without a word of explanation."

"Apparently, Zeke Boudreaux. It doesn't matter any longer. It's been months. Although..." Francesca's voice trailed off as she thought of the attention he'd been paying her.

"Although?"

Waving a hand in the air, she shook her head. "It's nothing. Regardless, it's over."

"And now you have Aaron showing an interest in you."

Francesca's eyes flew wide. "What? No. Aaron's a good man, but he's not for me. Besides, he's Edmund's business partner."

Nancy picked at the hem of her nightdress. "What does that have to do with you and Aaron?"

"For one, they're best friends. Plus, I have no interest in Aaron as more than a friend. I've no interest in anyone. However, I do believe you and Aaron would make an excellent match."

"Do you truly?"

Francesca couldn't miss the hopeful tone in Nancy's voice. "Yes, I do. This is the perfect opportunity for the two of you to become better acquainted, decide if you'll suit. It doesn't have to be left up to Aaron."

Nancy sat forward, clasping her hands in front of her. "You're right. Do you think Aaron is looking for marriage?"

"We haven't talked about it. I do believe he'd consider it if he met the right woman."

Nancy's initial excitement lessened at the words. "I suppose that's how it is for everyone, Frannie."

Francesca believed the same.

Zeke lay in bed, hands behind his head, thinking of Francesca. He'd been with her most of the day, and craved more time with her. Unfortunately, she wanted nothing to do with him. Not in the way he wanted.

Francesca had been firm in her refusal to carry on a conversation beyond the usual niceties. Polite and cordial without the warmth of when he'd been courting her. He'd expected the distance, not the cool indifference.

Zeke didn't blame her. Francesca's icy reaction was his fault. He'd created the distance, hurting her in unintended ways when he'd failed to explain why he'd backed away from their chance of being together.

Regret sliced through him. It hadn't taken too long to realize he'd made the greatest mistake of his life. Fear of commitment had given way to disgust with himself, then deep remorse.

Still, he'd failed to explain his actions. Zeke no longer had a choice. Starting tomorrow, everything between them was about to change.

Chapter Thirteen

Zeke and fellow deputy, Hawke DeBell, met Aaron at the mine early Monday morning. Searching the wreckage of the office, finding nothing useful, they and the manager had spent several hours speaking with a different group of miners.

A handful thought they'd seen someone near the office about an hour before the explosion, but no one could identify him as one of the other miners. Nor could they say for certain the man placed a charge.

They did agree he wore black pants, shirt, and hat, with a short beard and mustache. Two said he was tall, well over six feet, while the third disagreed, swearing he was several inches shorter. One said he had short hair, while the other two said it was long.

One miner did make a comment, which had hit Zeke square in the chest. The miner swore the man had a scar down his face, although he couldn't recall which side. No one could remember a minor with the same type of scar. Could it have been the same man who'd attacked Zeke, almost killing him?

"Did he have a Bowie knife?" he'd asked.

Stroking his beard, the miner had shaken his head. "Could've, but I didn't see one."

During the ride back to Splendor, he, Hawke, and Aaron had tossed out various reasons why someone would attack the office. They did agree the explosion had been set to cover up whatever had been taken.

Other than the weekly payroll and a few corporate documents, nothing of value was kept inside. The men had been paid before the manager rode to town, which ruled out the theft of payroll. As for the documents, copies were kept in the offices of their lawyer in New York and Splendor. Aaron had made sure Francesca O'Reilly had her own set tucked away in a file when arriving in town.

By the time they'd reached town, the men had been no closer to figuring out the reason for the explosion than before leaving the mine. Sharing the information with Gabe and several deputies had brought nothing. It didn't mean they'd give up on resolving why, and finding the person responsible.

Zeke left the jail, his chest tightening as he mentally reviewed what he planned next. Stopping at the entrance to the law office, he glanced around before stepping inside to take the stairs to the second floor.

He could hear the voices halfway up, hesitating a moment before continuing. Zeke had made up his mind to go through with his decision, no matter the obstacles.

Giving a sharp rap on the door, he turned the knob, peering inside. Francesca sat at her desk, Nancy looking over her shoulder at a document. The laughter stopped the instant the women noticed him hovering partway inside the office.

"Am I interrupting anything?" Not waiting for a response, he closed the door behind him, taking several steps forward.

Nancy shot him a cautious smile. "Frannie hired me as her secretary. I'm afraid I've a lot to learn."

"You're doing great." Francesca shifted her attention from Nancy to Zeke, her features holding little warmth. "Did you learn more about the explosion?"

"Some." He explained about the man a few of the miners had seen near the office. "We aren't giving up on finding whoever set the charge." Zeke didn't miss how Francesca watched him as he spoke, her gaze penetrating, moving over him in a slow perusal. The undisguised interest made his mouth go dry and curiosity rise. For a woman who insisted on indifference, her scrutiny indicated something else.

"If you don't have plans, would you accompany me to supper this evening, Frannie?"

Flushing, she fumbled with the paper before her. "I'm afraid—"

"She'd love to go with you, Deputy," Nancy answered for her.

"But—"

"Did you forget Aaron is taking me to supper at McCall's tonight, Frannie?"

Brows drawn together, she opened her mouth to reply, then closed it.

"Should I assume you're available?" Zeke didn't bother to hide a smirk.

"Well, I..."

"You have no other plans, Frannie. Why eat alone?" Nancy sent a conspiratorial glance at Zeke.

Satisfied the matter had been settled, Zeke retreated to the door. "I'll come to your house at six." Before she could object, he was out the door.

Shoving up, Frannie glared at her friend. "What were you thinking?"

A grin tipped the corners of Nancy's mouth. "That you could use an evening to relax with a handsome man."

"You know what happened between us."

"I also know you still care about him."

Francesca couldn't deny it. She hated wanting a man who'd hurt her, and probably would again if she let down her already fragile defenses. "It isn't wise for me to trust him again. There's no reason for him to invite me to supper."

"Unless he regrets what happened and wants to try again."

Focusing back on the paper before her, she snorted. "Doubtful. I think he feels guilty about how he ended the courtship. Taking me to supper is his way of apologizing."

Nancy studied her friend. The sadness she'd noticed when first arriving in Splendor hadn't diminished at all. Francesca may have thought she loved Edmund, but it was the rugged, gruff, and much too handsome deputy who owned her heart.

"Maybe it's more, Frannie."

As wonderful as that might be, she shook off the ridiculous notion. "It's not."

Picking up the sheath of papers she'd been reviewing with Frannie, Nancy turned toward the door. "At least you'll get a lovely supper. I want to hear all the details tonight."

Waiting until she left, Frannie dropped her face into her hands, groaning. Why had she allowed Nancy to push her into supper with Zeke? Since getting away from her controlling father, she'd worked hard to establish her independence, making decisions which suited her, and not because it was expected.

The one setback had been her experience with Zeke. Francesca didn't intend to make the same mistake twice. One supper and she'd never have to share a table with him again.

Zeke stopped in front of Francesca's house, brushing dust from his pants while glancing up and down the street. He couldn't dismiss the feeling of being watched, wondering if the man who'd attacked him, and possibly set the explosion at the mine office, was nearby.

The business owners in town had received his description, been told about the scar and Bowie knife. It had been weeks, and so far, he hadn't shown his face. Or he'd been able to hide his appearance well enough not to be recognized.

Shoving the man from his mind, he thought of the evening ahead with Francesca. He hadn't expected her to agree. If Nancy hadn't been present, he wouldn't be standing here tonight.

Moving to the front door, he rapped twice, taking a step back. He couldn't recall the last time he'd been so uncertain of anything. When the door opened, his breath caught at the sight before him.

"Good evening, Deputy." Zeke didn't miss the slight smirk touching her lips.

"Miss O'Reilly. You look stunning." A few months ago, she would've blushed, glanced away at the compliment. Tonight, her gaze met his straight on.

"Thank you. Let me get my wrap and we can go."

"Good evening, Zeke." He turned at Aaron's voice. "I didn't know you'd be visiting Francesca tonight."

"I'm escorting her to supper. I understand you're accompanying Nancy to McCall's."

Aaron stared at the front door, hesitating before walking up the steps. "I've known her a long time. However, I'm just beginning to see how much fun she can be. Even with the events in New York, she smiles, trying to make others feel better."

"You like her."

Aaron grinned. "I'm finding I do. Quite a great deal."

Both turned when the door opened. Francesca stepped outside, motioning for Aaron to enter. "Nancy is almost ready. She's excited about tonight, so don't spoil it."

Zeke held his tongue while Aaron looked aghast at the comment. "I'd never do anything to upset her."

"Well, I've given my warning." She ignored Zeke's outstretched hand to help her down the steps. "I'm ready."

He had the odd impulse to ask Francesca if she truly wanted to go to supper with him, but remained silent. Zeke needed to explain, and this might be his one chance.

Seeing the stubbornness on her face, he held out his arm, not budging until she relented, slipping her hand through it. They walked in silence through the quiet streets toward the St. James and its Eagle's Nest restaurant.

"Thank you, Thomas." Zeke nodded at their maître d' before pulling out Francesca's chair, then seating himself.

"Would you care for wine?" Thomas had been at the Eagle's Nest since it opened, and had proven his value many times.

"A glass for both of us." Zeke watched Francesca, not liking the way she stared at the clenched hands in her lap. She'd always been vivacious, speaking about any and all topics. Tonight wasn't one of those times.

"I believe you brought me here to talk. So..." She motioned with her hand for him to speak.

Waiting for Thomas to set down the wine and take their orders, Zeke lifted his glass toward her. "To a good evening."

Francesca picked up her glass with a controlled nod, saying nothing as she tipped it toward him. Taking a sip, she set the glass down. An expectant look crossed her face, letting him know there'd be no more delays in their conversation.

"First, I'm sorry about how I stopped calling on you, Frannie. It was never my intention to hurt you."

She shrugged, as if it no longer mattered.

Forcing himself not to drain the glass of wine and request more, he cleared his throat. "I was a coward, Frannie. There's no other word for what I did."

"Didn't do," Francesca whispered, and she was right.

"Yes..." He blew out. "I should've explained my hesitation at continuing our relationship."

"There was no hesitation, Zeke. You ignored me, stopped calling on me, and began spending your time with other women."

Wincing, he picked up his glass, then set it down, his voice a low growl. "There were no other women, Frannie. Not then, and not now."

A long breath left her lungs before she looked away.

"After getting to know you, I came to understand I'm not the kind of man you need."

Her head whipped back toward him, eyes blazing in anger. "What do you mean, '*Not the kind of man I need*'? What you mean is I'm not the kind of woman *you want*.

I'm quiet, boring, and not at all suitable for a man such as yourself," she huffed out. "At least you can be honest." Pulling the napkin, she tried to toss it on the table when Zeke's hand clamped down on her wrist.

"Don't go, Frannie. I'm not explaining this well." He shook his head. "Not at all."

Hesitating a moment, she lowered herself back into the chair. "Explain to me about you not being good enough for me."

They waited while Thomas set their plates in front of them. "May I pour more wine?"

"Yes." Zeke held up his glass. After Thomas left, he stared at the wine, rolling the stem between his fingers. "I didn't stop seeing you because you're boring or quiet. You're neither. What you are is the most remarkable woman I've ever had the privilege to know."

Brows drawing together, she took a small bite of potatoes, confused at his comment.

Zeke picked up his fork, staring at the plate filled with steak and mashed potatoes. "The truth is I'm a deputy in a small town in the frontier of Montana. I don't own a home and have little savings. I don't see a time in the future where either will improve, Frannie." Looking past her through the window to the street, he shook his head. "You're beautiful, educated, cultured, with social standing I will never achieve. I'm an ex-Confederate soldier and lawman. No one special. You deserve a man who can provide much more than me."

Features changing from confused to angry, she set down the fork, squaring her shoulders. "That is the most absurd reason I've ever heard."

Chapter Fourteen

Absurd? How could Francesca not understand? Brows rising, his gaze narrowed on her. "It's the truth, Frannie. After you spend time to consider my reasons, you'll see I'm right."

"And here I thought you were a smart man." Grabbing her fork, she stabbed a piece of roast. Chewing and swallowing, she pointed the fork at him. "If that's the best you can do for an excuse, it's pure pitiful. I'm no better than you. I've spoken with Hex, and know the two of you came from wealth and were well educated."

"We lost it all in the war."

"You didn't lose your brains, and that's what seems to be in jeopardy." Francesca scooped up potatoes, stuffing them into her mouth in an angry gesture, which would've made him laugh if she wasn't so irritated. Swallowing, she took a sip of wine, letting out a calming breath. "I'm going to finish my meal, then return home. When you're ready to offer the truth, you'll know where to find me."

Not glancing his way, she didn't see the wide eyes or stunned expression on his face. "Are you telling me you don't care that I'm not good enough for you?"

Head turning to look at him, her mouth twisted in disbelief. "To be clear, I'm *not* better than you. My life is here in Splendor. I practice law, fix my own meals, do my own laundry, and spend the free time I have visiting with friends. I'm saving to purchase a horse and buy one of Noah's houses. It's ludicrous for anyone to think I'm better than them. Especially you. I thought you knew me better than that."

"Frannie..."

Holding up her hand, she stopped him. "I'm too angry to talk more right now." Pushing her plate away, she touched the corners of her mouth with the napkin as Thomas walked up. "I'll have coffee, please. And a piece of whatever May Covington baked today."

"And what may I get you, Deputy Boudreaux?"

Jaw tight, Zeke glared up at Thomas, causing the young man to take a step back. "The same. Except bring me two of what May made."

"Uh...yes, sir."

Leaning back in his chair, Zeke stared at Francesca, his mind whirling. "I should've said something months ago."

"Yes, you should have."

"I'm not lying about the reason, Frannie."

"Too bad, because it's preposterous."

Leaning his head back, he stared at the ceiling. "I was a fool."

She shot him a quick glance before smiling at Thomas as he approached with their coffee and dessert. "Yes, you were."

He blew out a low curse, shocking both Francesca and Thomas. Shaking his head, Zeke grimaced. "Sorry. That was inappropriate."

"It does happen, Deputy." Thomas couldn't hide a grin as he walked away.

Cutting into his first piece of peach pie, he chanced a look at Francesca. "Would it be too much to ask if we can start again, Frannie?"

Taking her time with her bite of pie, she swallowed it down with coffee. "May makes the best desserts."

His chest tightened at her lack of an answer. "Yes, she does."

"Does she ever bring any to the jail for her husband?"

"Caleb regularly brings a tray of her baked goods to share." His frustration grew, but he kept it to himself.

"I should ask if I can pay her to make a pie for me."

"I'm certain she would, Frannie." Continuing to wait, he finished one piece of pie and started the second. If necessary, he'd escort her home and stay until she gave him an answer. He didn't have to wait.

"I don't know, Zeke." Wary green eyes met his deep brown ones, the sadness he saw punching him in the gut. "What happened before..." She looked away, her mouth pulled into a thin line.

"You don't trust me."

Francesca gave a slight shake of her head. "No, Zeke. I don't."

Answering with a slow nod, he signaled to Thomas for their bill before escorting her outside. "Will you take a walk with me, Frannie?"

For a moment, he thought she would refuse. Her faced tipped up to meet his gaze. "All right. I could use the fresh air."

They took the boardwalk toward the boardinghouse, stopping in front of the new Emporium to look into the large front window. Josephine Lucero, rancher Dom Lucero's wife, and Olivia McCord, the doctor's wife, opened it to provide items not available at Stan Petermann's general store. Reverend Paige's wife, Ruth, worked a few hours each week, her main job being to update the front window. Sales had increased right after her first design scheme.

"Ruth is so creative with the window display." Francesca's wide gaze moved over the items, landing on a beautifully crafted leather piece of luggage.

Chuckling, Zeke tried to see what Francesca did. "I suppose."

"You have to admit, it does catch your attention."

Tilting his head one way, then the other, his mouth twisted into a rueful grin. "It's a little hard for a man to get excited about a lacy dress, wide-brimmed hat, luggage, world globe, and parasol."

"Don't forget the wide spray of pine branches." She glanced up at him, lips twitching.

He controlled his desire to laugh. "I'll admit that is a nice touch. Are you ready to move on?"

In answer, she turned toward the boardinghouse. Passing two vacant stores and the raucous sounds from

Finn's saloon, they stopped in front of the newspaper office.

"It's hard to believe this building was leveled by an explosion not long ago." Francesca's attention fixed on the large printing press just inside. Behind it were two desks and a long counter. She knew ink and other supplies filled the back room.

"The town came together to rebuild it within a couple weeks."

"I'd arrived in town from New York days before," Francesca said.

"I remember." Zeke recalled the day he'd spotted her on the boardwalk, along with four other friends of Rachel Pelletier. He'd been fascinated with her since that first day. "You were the prettiest woman I'd ever seen."

Swallowing the hard ball of regret in her throat, she didn't mention her own instant attraction to him. Never had she felt a tug on her heart as had happened when her gaze landed on the broad-shouldered, ruggedly handsome deputy. Her heart had begun its own rhythm, and even after all these months, it hadn't stopped beating for him.

Tugging her from the view of the printing press, he continued past the Dixie, which was packed every evening, but without the rowdiness of Finn's. He thought of Dahlia's drawing of the brand, which had been stolen by the man who'd attacked him. Fearing for her life, Dahlia had refused to draw a second one.

"Did you ever learn anything from the brand?" Francesca asked.

"I was just thinking about the brand. Dahlia wouldn't draw a second one. She thought whoever clubbed me would come after her. I did describe it to Noah, but he didn't recall one similar."

Brows drawing together, she gave a slow nod. "You're left with the scar and Bowie knife."

"We passed the information to those in town. So far, nothing."

Not stopping to look inside the Assay Office, they glanced into the boardinghouse before Zeke led her toward the creek. The flow had decreased during the warm summer months. The winter would bring rain and snow, raising the water level.

Years before, Noah Brandt had built a bench, installing it near the edge of the creek not far from the school. "Would you care to sit down?"

"No. If you don't mind, I'd rather stand." She tugged her wrap tighter around her shoulders, moving away from him to stop by the creek. "Did you truly stop seeing me because you believed you weren't good enough?"

Zeke didn't want to start another heated argument. He also wouldn't lie. "Yes. A part of me still believes it."

"If that's true, then there's no reason for us to try again. It would be best to maintain a friendship."

Walking up to stand behind her, Zeke placed his hands on her waist. "Your friendship is important to me, Frannie."

Feeling a flush creep up her neck and face, she considered stepping away. His hands on her felt too good, and it had been so long since she'd felt his touch. Slipping her arm through his for a walk through town didn't come close to the shivers running up and down her spine now. Tightening his grip on her waist, he bent to whisper next to her ear.

"Give me a chance, Frannie. A week, a month, however long it takes to prove how much I want to do this right the second time."

The man's charms had been obvious since their first introduction. His deep, caressing voice had always drawn her to him. Tonight, they began to crack her defenses. Remembering how he'd hurt her, she took several steps away, keeping her back to him.

"I don't know, Zeke. It's taken you months to explain why you stopped calling on me. Besides the occasional greeting on the street, you never took even a few minutes to talk with me." Turning to face him, a shadow crossed her features. "Perhaps there's another reason you lost interest."

Taking a step toward her, he held out his open hands. "There was one, and only one, reason. You deserve a much better man than me." He moved a few inches closer. "Even though I'll always believe that, I'm selfish, Frannie. I want you in my life."

Clasping her hands together, she searched his gaze. Hex had always said his younger brother could mask his feelings, but she saw the honesty on his face.

"For how long?" Shifting to walk along the water's edge, she stared into the ever darkening night, not hearing him come up beside her.

Taking her arm, he turned her to face him. "I won't make the same mistake twice. Give me another chance and I'll prove it to you."

Before she could respond, he lowered his mouth to hers.

Francesca lay on her side of the bed, staring at the ceiling as she had been for hours. She could still feel the seductive tingle of Zeke's lips on hers, the way his arms banded around her. Too soon, he'd stepped back, both breathing heavily after the brief contact.

Glancing to her side, she smiled at Nancy. She'd already been asleep in bed when Zeke escorted her back home. Francesca hoped her best friend and Aaron had a wonderful time at McCall's. If given time, she felt certain they'd realize there could be a future for them. Francesca wasn't so certain about her and Zeke.

She didn't know if it was the sincerity on his face and in his voice, or the kiss which created a heat she could still feel. Francesca supposed it didn't matter.

By the time they'd returned to her front door, she'd agreed to give him a second chance...with conditions. First, they would not refer to their time together as *courting*. Instead, they'd be two friends sharing a meal, a stroll, or a ride. Second, if either decided marriage was not in their future, they'd explain before walking away.

And last, Francesca insisted they could each spend time with other men and women.

Chapter Fifteen

Zeke sat in his living room well after midnight, tossing back a second shot of whiskey. The initial elation he'd felt at getting a second chance had been tempered by his agreement to Francesca's condition about spending time with other men. Granted, he could share time with other women, but he didn't want anyone else. He wanted Francesca.

Zeke understood her reasons for the request. The most important being her lack of trust in him. He didn't like it, but couldn't blame her.

Zeke had heard she'd turned down offers of supper or lunch from other men. Starting tomorrow, he'd make certain everyone in Splendor had no doubt of his claim on her.

A sharp knock on the door had him sitting up. "What the hell..." Barefoot, he plodded to the front door, sweeping it open. "Hex. Do you know what time it is?"

"Unfortunately, yes, since I'm working your shift." He stomped past Zeke, lowering himself onto the sofa. "I saw your light and decided you were still awake." Eyeing the bottle of whiskey on the table. "How was your evening with Frannie?"

"You came by after midnight to question me about my social life?" Zeke walked back to his chair, lifting the bottle off the table. "A drink?"

"A small one. I have to move on in a few minutes." Hex lifted a brow. "Frannie?"

Handing him a glass, Zeke slumped into his chair. "What would you do if Chrissy was agreeable to court you as long as she could see other men?"

Choking on his whiskey, Hex straightened. "I'd tell her it wouldn't happen. Is that what she wants?"

"For now." Sipping a small pour, he rolled it around in his mouth before swallowing. "She doesn't trust that I'm serious about courting her a second time. It's what she wants, so..." Shrugging, he tossed back the rest of his drink.

Leaning forward, Hex rested his arms on his knees. "Is there a man you don't know about?"

Pressing his thumb and forefinger against his eyes, Zeke shook his head. "She's protecting herself from getting hurt again. Walking away was the biggest mistake of my life."

"Can't argue with you." Taking the last swallow of whiskey, Hex stood. "Are you able to see other women?"

"Yeah."

"Do you plan to?"

"Not interested." Standing, he joined his brother at the door. "There's just one woman I want."

Settling a hand on Zeke's shoulder, Hex squeezed. "Give it time. Frannie's cautious. She's also smart. According to Chrissy, her feelings for you run deep. She's skittish, much like a horse who's been mistreated."

Zeke winced at the comparison. He'd never meant to hurt her.

"Spend time with her. Be the man you were before walking away."

Closing the door behind Hex, he blew out a tired breath. His brother was right. He had few options if he wanted to build a life with Frannie. Give her time while being there.

Skirting between two buildings, Francesca opened the door to the law offices. There were three on the bottom floor and another three on the second. When she'd arrived in Splendor, there'd been one attorney.

Ernest Payson returned after the death of his brother, Albert, another lawyer. Staying to keep the practice going, he'd been thrilled to welcome Francesca. Although accepted in town, his heart belonged back east. A few months passed before he made her a proposal she'd found impossible to resist.

Ernest would transfer his clients to her for the price of passage back to Boston. Within a few days, Francesca had become the only attorney in Splendor. It hadn't taken long for her to determine the town required another one.

Taking the stairs to her office, she thought of the telegrams she'd sent to various towns, east and west.

She'd received a few replies, one that appeared promising.

Setting her reticule aside, she removed the hat purchased not long after arriving in town. Shunning the conventional bonnet, she'd selected a wide-brimmed hat with a low crown worn by some ranch hands. It may be considered unstylish for a woman, but Francesca loved it.

Withdrawing Beauty's letter and telegram from the safe, she reviewed them, making notes. There was no proof Louis Elder had sent the telegram, and the letter held the thoughts of a young woman who feared for her freedom.

The deputy in Big Pine had confirmed no wanted poster for Beauty existed. It didn't mean she wasn't in danger. The threatening telegram made it clear someone wanted her gone. Bernie Griggs verified the message had been sent from Kansas City, where Kyle Forshew died and Louis Elder still lived. An assumption Francesca wanted to confirm.

She'd sent her own telegram right after her first meeting with Beauty. This one to Allan Pinkerton. They'd met on more than one occasion at social events when he'd visited New York for business. Her former employer, a well-known attorney, had introduced them. Unlike some big city dwellers who disapproved of his methods, she found him refreshing, ready and willing to do what was required to bring in those accused of crimes.

Impatient for Pinkerton's report, Francesca kept busy studying Beauty's documents, and her work for other clients. Setting aside the letter and telegram, she picked up the draft of a purchase contract for a business Gabe Evans and Nick Barnett were considering. The largest hotel in Big Pine was floundering, which presented an ideal opportunity to do business in the territorial capital.

Immersing herself in the document, she almost missed the rap on her door. Before she could respond, the door opened.

"Zeke. What are you doing here?" Wincing at her less than cordial welcome, she stood, attempting to ignore the way her heart rate doubled in his presence.

Without answering, he took his time crossing the few feet to stand a few inches away. Lifting a hand, Zeke hesitated an instant before stroking the backs of his fingers down her cheek. When she didn't back away, he slipped his hand behind her neck, drawing her closer.

"I've wanted to do this since waking up this morning." Brushing his lips across hers, he kissed her deeply before lifting his head. "Perfect."

"Whaaat?" Glassy eyes met his, her cheeks showing the effect he had on her.

"You're perfect, Frannie," he whispered, kissing her again before stepping away. "Let me escort you to lunch."

"Lunch?" She shook off the incredible feeling of his lips against hers.

"It's noon. Have you eaten?"

She moved back to her chair, creating distance. "No, but I do have work to finish."

He followed her steps, staying within a foot of her. "We can go downstairs to McCall's or the boardinghouse. Whatever is most convenient for you."

Inching away, she steadied herself on the edge of the desk. "I can't take much time, Zeke."

"I understand, Frannie. Shall we?" He motioned to the door as Nancy walked in, holding several papers.

"Oh. I didn't know you had a visitor." She gave Zeke a warm smile. Much more welcoming than Francesca.

"I'm taking Frannie to lunch. Would you care to join us?"

Placing the papers on the desk, Nancy shook her head. "Thank you, but I have plans with Aaron. These are what you requested Frannie. If you have time this afternoon, I'd prefer to go over them with you."

"We won't be gone long, Nancy. Let's meet when you return with Aaron, since he must review the documents, also."

"That would be fine. Enjoy yourselves." Nancy gave a slight wave before leaving them alone.

Zeke lifted a brow, indicating the door. "Are you ready?"

Francesca stared out the window of the boardinghouse restaurant at the telegraph office, which also served as the town's post office and stagecoach stop. From what she'd learned, Bernie Griggs had been the clerk since the building first opened. Hearing the server set down their meals, she turned her attention to Zeke.

"Have you learned anything more about the explosion at the mine?"

"From what Hawke, Aaron, and I learned when we went back on Monday, everything points to one of the miners setting the charge."

"Why?"

Zeke lifted one shoulder in a shrug. "He was vocal about his dislike of the man Aaron hired as the new manager, and he knows how to handle dynamite. He hasn't been seen since the explosion."

She didn't appear impressed. "None of it means he's the one who blew up the office."

"Maybe not. Aaron will continue to investigate, as will the manager. He'll let me or Gabe know if they learn anything more. In the meantime, they're rebuilding the office. The manager also posted guards."

Francesca nodded, turning to look out the window at the same time the stage from Big Pine arrived. "Have you ever thought of leaving Splendor?"

"Vaguely," Zeke responded.

Her head whipped back toward him. "What does that mean?"

"Hex and my niece are here. His marriage to Chrissy has changed his plans, as well as mine."

"So, you're staying?" She needed him to say it, to know he felt the tug of this small town as much as she did.

"Yes. Unless there's a good reason for me to leave."

Her heart squeezed at the thought of him leaving. "Such as what?"

"If you decided this wasn't where you wanted to live." At her stunned expression, he pushed his plate away. "I want to build a life with you, Frannie. I'm hoping it will be in Splendor."

"How can you know your feelings for me, Zeke? After what happened, how can I believe *you*?"

"Isn't that the reason we're spending time together? You wanted time to decide whether or not you can trust me again."

Rather than responding, Francesca stared out the window. The stage driver slapped the lines, leaving for his next stop. When the coach rolled away, a lone man stood on the boardwalk, two pieces of luggage at his feet.

She watched his gaze move up and down the street, as if deciding what to do next. Dressed in dark trousers, vest, and white shirt, his coat was draped over one arm, a black Homburg hat perched on his head. She saw no visible weapon, not doubting the man had one stashed in his luggage. Few men traveled west without some kind of protection.

He appeared to be in his thirties, close to six feet tall, slender, with a full mustache and ruddy complexion. From this distance, she couldn't tell the color of his hair, assuming it was dark.

"Do you know him?"

Francesca's head jerked toward Zeke. "No. At least, I don't believe so. There's something about him that's familiar." She glanced out the window again, then gave a quick shake of her head. "I'm certain I've never met him." Yet something niggled at her. Her thoughts went to Beauty and the telegram from Kansas City. "I should return to my office."

Without comment, Zeke signaled the server and paid for their meals before escorting her outside. He noticed her attention had returned to the man walking toward the St. James Hotel, a piece of luggage in each hand.

"Do you want to speak with him, Frannie?"

Looking up at him, her brows drew together. "Who?"

"The passenger from the stage. Your interest in him is obvious."

"I have *no* interest in the man. Well, there may be a slight bit of curiosity." No matter how much Francesca wanted Zeke's opinion, she couldn't betray the confidential nature of her meetings with Beauty, including the letter and telegram secured in her safe.

"It appears he'll be checking into the St. James. If you're interested, I can ask about him."

Gripping Zeke's arm, she squeezed it. "Please don't. As I said, it's mere curiosity. He seems so out of place in Splendor."

Chuckling, he covered her hand with his. "So did you when you first arrived." Ignoring her irritated huff, he turned her to face him. His gaze moved over her simple cotton dress, flat shoes, and western hat. "You fit in fine now, darlin'."

She bit her lip, as if considering a major decision. "Do you work tonight?"

"I'm back on my regular schedule. I'll relieve Hex at five."

"Would you be interested in supper with Nancy and me before then? Four o'clock, at my house?"

Unable to hide a grin, he brushed a kiss across her cheek. "I'd enjoy that, Frannie." Crossing the street, he stopped in front of her office.

"Thank you for lunch, Zeke. I had a wonderful time."

"My pleasure. I'll see you in a few hours." He stayed on the boardwalk outside her office while she entered and walked up the stairs.

Turning, his gaze lit on the front of the St. James. Francesca's curiosity about the newcomer had caught Zeke's interest, triggering warning signals up and down his spine. No matter what she'd said, there was more to the stranger than she wanted him to believe.

Chapter Sixteen

Francesca walked straight to her safe, removing the documents Beauty had entrusted to her. Sitting down, she spread them out on her desk, grabbing the notes she'd made earlier. Scanning the telegram first, not finding what she sought, she set it aside. Examining the letter, her attention focused on a short description of Louis Elder.

Slender. Dark hair. Mustache. About six feet tall. Spotty red complexion. Normally wears dark clothing.

Francesca's gaze then landed on the last item on the list.

Dark, Homburg hat.

She had little time to consider the information before hearing a soft knock. Gathering the papers, she slid them into a drawer before walking to the door and opening it.

A man in his thirties, close to six feet tall and slender, with thinning dark hair and full mustache, stared back at her. In his hand, he nervously fingered the edges of a Homburg hat. Her throat constricted. *The man from the stagecoach.*

"May I help you?"

"Are you Francesca O'Reilly, the lawyer?"

"Yes."

"Excellent. I'm Louis Elder, and I need your help."

The name hit her square in the chest. Louis Elder, the man Beauty believed sent her the threatening telegram, and the man arriving by stage were one and the same. Hiding the wave of contempt at facing the man, she stepped aside.

"Please, come in."

Closing the door, she motioned toward a chair. "Please sit down and tell me how I can help you."

"I'm searching for someone, and thought you might be able to assist me."

Lowering herself into the chair, she sat forward. "Why are you looking for him?"

"That's my business."

"Not if you want me to help you, Mr. Elder."

Pursing his lips, Louis stared at her a moment before chuckling. "All right. I believe she murdered a friend of mine."

"*She*?"

"Women do kill people, Miss O'Reilly."

"I'm well aware of that. Do you have a wanted poster on her?" She recalled her communications with the deputy in Big Pine, confirming he couldn't find anything on Beauty.

"No," he bit out. "There wasn't enough proof for the Kansas City sheriff or local judge to approve one."

"Yet you've traveled all the way to Splendor because you believe otherwise. Even if you find her, the local sheriff won't arrest her without proof. The fact you didn't have enough to warrant a wanted poster will go against you."

Elder flicked a hand in the air, waving off her comment. "If I can locate her, I'll be able to obtain a confession."

She became more uncomfortable with each of his answers, but wanted as much information as possible before he left. "Exactly who do you believe she murdered?"

"My half brother, Kyle Forshew."

Brows drawing together, she rested her arms on the desk. "I thought you said she'd killed a friend."

"Yes, yes. Kyle and I were also friends." It was a lie that came easily. Even sharing a father never made them close. Louis rubbed his forehead, recalling he and Kyle's shared past.

Their father was married to Kyle's mother when he had an affair, resulting in Louis's birth. He was a son the oldest Forshew refused to acknowledge. It had come as a surprise when he'd died of heart failure, leaving Louis a moderate bank account and house in Kansas City. By then, both of their mothers had also passed. Kyle had decided not to contest the insignificant amount going to his half brother.

After Kyle's death, Louis had been certain the fortune would pass to him. He'd been shocked to learn his half brother's estate had passed to Nellie Crawford. It hadn't taken Louis long to learn it was Beauty's given name.

Kyle's lawyer continued to search for his client's mistress, expending little money or effort to find her. Louis had been more aggressive, locating her in Splendor after a few months.

"Mr. Elder?"

He looked at Francesca as if he'd forgotten her presence, then blinked to clear his head. "Apologies."

"It's quite all right. Why do you believe she's the one to have killed him?"

Settling back in the chair, he crossed a leg over his thigh. "Kyle had taken her on a ride to the river. His body was found the following morning, the carriage gone."

Francesca nodded. So far, the story matched what Beauty had told her, as well as the details in her letter about the events. Apparently, Louis didn't know about Kyle ending their relationship for the company of a younger woman.

"Do you have any idea if they argued or had a conversation which would anger her enough to leave him behind?"

"His lawyer did mention something to me."

"And what was that, Mr. Elder?"

"Kyle had met with him the previous week about some property in town he wanted to purchase. At the same time, he mentioned needing to change some of his personal documents, as he planned to end his relationship with his current mistress. He'd met someone else and wanted to make provisions for both women."

"I see." No matter how many similar stories she heard, Francesca would never understand the ease at which some men moved from one woman to another.

"I believe Kyle told her what he intended and she killed him, took the carriage, and left town."

"But neither the sheriff nor judge believed your theory."

"No. There was a couple who swore they saw Kyle at the river after she arrived back in town. I'm certain they were mistaken."

Not responding right away, she considered her options. Francesca wouldn't endanger Beauty, but neither would she miss the opportunity to learn more about Louis and his deceased half brother.

"I'm sorry, Mr. Elder. I won't help you locate an innocent woman, then force a confession from her. The fact is, if she is here, you don't need my help. Splendor isn't a big town."

His friendly manner vanished, features hardening into a scowl. "You don't want to turn me down, Miss O'Reilly. I will pay well for your help."

Standing, she went straight to the door, opening it. "As I said, you'd do better looking for the woman yourself."

Shoving from the chair, he walked to within inches of her. "Don't you want to know her name?"

"It's not necessary."

"Perhaps you've heard of her. Nellie Crawford, but everyone calls her Beauty."

Zeke stiffened, lowering his hat to cover his face when the man from the stage entered Francesca's building. Deciding to wait, he lowered himself onto a bench on the opposite side of the street. The time passed slower than pouring molasses in the winter.

After fifteen minutes, he couldn't take the waiting any longer. Halfway across the street, the man exited her office, glanced around, then disappeared into the bank. Zeke continued to her office, opening the door as a figure slipped out the back door.

"Where are you going, Frannie?" Hurrying to the door, he cracked it open, watching as she walked the short distance to Ruby's Palace, took a quick look around, then slipped inside.

Following, he hesitated several minutes before straightening his hat and pushing open the front door. Waiting a moment for his eyes to adjust to the dark, he scanned the room, spotting her sitting alone at a small table to his right.

When Ruby saw him, he touched a finger to his lips, nodding toward Francesca. Lifting her chin in response, she walked to the table and sat down. A moment later, Ruby stood, motioning one of the girls over. Whispering in the young woman's ear, she made a shooing sound before her employee turned to race up the stairs.

Zeke slipped along the wall, getting as close to the table as he could without Francesca noticing him.

Ruby leaned toward Francesca. "Are you sure you don't want a drink, honey? You seem a little piqued."

"No, thank you. I just need to speak with Beauty for a few minutes, then I'll be on my way." Her gaze landed on the almost ethereal figure of Nellie Crawford float down the stairs.

Standing, Ruby gave Beauty a stern look. "Ten minutes and no more."

"Of course, Miss Ruby." Waiting until the older woman left, Beauty took a quick look around before sitting beside Francesca. "I'm surprised to see you here."

"It's important."

Beauty's features stilled as she gripped her hands together. "What is it?"

"Louis Elder came in on today's stage."

Already pale, all the color drained from her face. "Are you sure?"

"He came to my office and introduced himself. Louis is looking for you, Beauty."

"I don't understand. Why would he meet with you?"

Francesca shifted to see Ruby watching them. "He wanted to hire me to find you."

"Why?" The word came out before Beauty could stop it.

"Louis didn't say, but I believe he doesn't want to go to the sheriff."

Beauty offered a slow nod, not responding.

"He admitted there isn't a wanted poster. The sheriff and judge in Kansas City agreed he didn't have proof you were responsible," Francesca said. "I believe Louis doesn't want to draw attention to himself, so he wanted to hire me."

Lips trembling, she gripped the edge of the table. "What did you tell him?"

"No, of course. You're my client, Beauty." Francesca's mouth drew into a stern line. "There's got to be another reason for him to be in Splendor."

"What do you mean?"

"Louis admits he has no proof you did anything wrong, so he can't expect Sheriff Evans to arrest you. As you know, the trip from Kansas City is long and tiring. There must be another reason for him traveling all this way." Francesca looked up at the sound of men's voices. "I can't stay any longer. Don't go outside the Palace unless you're with someone. And do not go to the St. James. That's where Louis is staying."

"Good afternoon, ladies."

Both women jumped at Zeke's voice, Francesca's chair tipping over when she hurried to stand. "What are you doing here?"

"Making certain you're both safe."

"I—"

Pulling out a chair, he motioned to hers. "Please, sit down, Frannie. We have some talking to do."

Chapter Seventeen

Redemption's Edge Ranch

Billy shifted in the saddle, his gaze scanning the herd of cattle, watching for strays. He'd been in the same location for hours, without having to chase a single head. His back and shoulders ached as if he were forty instead of twenty-two.

Staring across the open pasture at another of the ranch hands, he blew out a slow breath, allowing his mind to shift to another day. It seemed as if months had passed, when it had been a few weeks since visiting the Blackfoot village. Less than a month since the Crow attack, and the death of the brave Shining Star had planned to marry.

She'd been devastated, buried in her own personal grief. Billy had felt helpless, an outsider who wouldn't have been allowed to offer comfort. Not that she would've accepted anything from him. Shining Star had a heart for one man, and he'd been murdered by the renegade band of Crow.

Pressing the palm of his hand to his chest, Billy tried to erase the images of a grieving, young woman. She'd been inconsolable as she walked alongside those carrying the body of her fallen brave. Her grief had been painful for him to watch.

When the men prepared to ride back to Redemption's Edge, he'd considered staying behind. The idea faded, comprehending Running Bear and his people wouldn't welcome his help. Taking care of their dead was limited to those who belonged.

"Billy!" Bull's shout forced him back to the present.

Turning to look behind him, he spotted one of the ranch's two foremen riding toward him. Reining his horse around, he waited for Bull to join him.

"Any problems with the herd?"

Billy's mouth twisted as he shook his head. "None. They're as quiet as I've ever seen them."

Chuckling, Bull reached over to clasp Billy on the shoulder. "Enjoy it while you can."

Both fell silent, their ever-watchful gazes scanning the herd. There were five Pelletier ranch hands guarding the herd of two hundred cattle.

Half a mile away, a small herd of longhorn cows purchased from Dom Lucero grazed. A Hereford bull, in a small corral near the main barn, waited to join them. The Pelletiers and Dom were experimenting with crossbreeding in the hope of creating more robust animals requiring less grazing land. So far, the results were encouraging.

Billy was curious about the new endeavor. Most days, he worked with Travis Dixon, breaking horses for Army contracts, training others for individual buyers. He'd learned a great deal from Travis since the Pelletiers had brought Billy and the other orphans to the ranch.

The work challenged him. More than once, Travis, and both Pelletiers, Dax and Luke, had commented how he was a natural with horses.

A whistle from across the pasture drew their attention. Tat, a man who'd been at the ranch as long as Bull, waved his arms while pointing north. Turning, their gazes landed on a small group of riders. It took a moment before they recognized the two riding in front.

Bull glanced at Billy. "It's Running Bear and his grandson, Swift Bear."

Billy's heart rate increased, seeing the other riders. "Who's with them?"

Pulling binoculars from his saddlebag, Bull focused on the approaching group. After a moment, he lowered the glasses, casting a wary glance at Billy. "I only recognize one of them."

"Who?"

"Shining Star."

"I'm so glad you and your friends were able to join us, Frannie." Rachel Pelletier's smile stretched across her face. "The idea for supper came to me when I heard about your friend arriving from New York." Rachel glanced at her. "And the death of her father."

Francesca continued to set the table, including spots for Nancy, Aaron, and Zeke. It felt good to get out of Splendor for several hours. "She's considering staying in

Splendor. Nancy's already spoken to Noah Brandt about renting one of his empty homes."

"That's wonderful news."

"Yes, it is." As excited as she was at the possibility Nancy would stay, Francesca's thoughts were on the day before, and the talk with Zeke.

Beauty hadn't wanted to confide in the deputy. It had taken a good amount of persuasion for Francesca to convince her Zeke would do all he could to help. When finished at Ruby's, they'd walked to the jail to speak with Gabe. The same as Zeke, he'd listened to both women without interrupting, asking a number of questions when they were done.

The sheriff had promised to speak with Louis Elder, check the wanted posters in his desk, and send a telegram to Sheriff Parker Sterling in Big Pine. He'd also planned to send another telegram to the sheriff in Kansas City.

Before they'd left the jail, Gabe and Zeke spoke among themselves, deciding to post a deputy at Ruby's to protect Beauty. They believed it unlikely Louis would attack her there, but given all they'd heard from the women, it would be the smart decision.

The following morning, a rider brought an invitation from Rachel to the Pelletiers' home that afternoon. The women welcomed the opportunity. At first, Zeke had balked at being included before relenting. He'd been to the ranch a few times, never staying long.

"Are you and Zeke..." Rachel's voice trailed off, knowing Francesca got her meaning.

"No. Well...in a way, we are seeing each other. Just not in the normal sense." She explained their unconventional agreement, surprised when Rachel laughed.

"You've always been a bit unconventional, Frannie. Defying your parents to train as a lawyer, moving across country, and now being courted by more than one man. I don't believe I've ever heard of any woman who desired such a unique situation."

Feeling her face flush, Francesca shook her head. "I'm not seeing anyone except Zeke."

Rachel's features warmed. "I know. What he did to you was cruel. I'm surprised you offered him a second chance."

"So am I." Frannie pulled out a chair, lowering herself onto it. "He's apologized for his behavior."

"That's something, I suppose." Rachel sat next to her, glancing out the front window to see Aaron and Nancy on the porch swing. Out by the barn, Zeke spoke with Dax. "I do believe he's a good man. There must've been a reason for his objectionable action."

Following Rachel's gaze outside, Francesca's attention focused on Zeke. "He convinced himself he wasn't good enough for me."

Staring at her for a moment, Rachel's brows drew together. "Why would he think that?"

Throwing up her hands in frustration, she blew out a frustrated breath. "I'm a lawyer, come from money, and deserve better than a deputy who has little to offer. No home of his own or a bank account that's worth much." Her mouth twisted into a wry grin. "I believe that covers it."

"Oh my." Rachel leaned back, rubbing her hands on the skirt of her dress.

"Did you know his family had wealth before he and Hex left to join the Confederate Army?"

"I'd heard as much. According to Dax, their father wasn't able to keep up his business during the war."

Frannie nodded. "Zeke and Hex tried to revive it, without success."

"Perhaps that's why he feels as if he doesn't deserve you. His side lost the war, then he lost the family business. Two severe blows in a short period of time. Zeke may have seen you as unattainable."

"If he thought that, why did he ask to court me?"

A grin tipped the corners of Rachel's mouth. "Because you're the woman he wants, Frannie."

The sound of voices preceded Aaron, Nancy, Zeke, and Dax entering the house, all four talking as they walked to the dining room.

"How can I help?" Nancy asked, joining Rachel and Francesca.

"Supper is ready to put on the table." Entering the kitchen, Rachel nodded to a platter of sliced roast, a bowl of mashed potatoes, and another holding vegetables. "Just those three."

"Smells wonderful." Nancy slid her hands under the platter. Returning to the dining room, she almost tripped at the sound of the front door slamming. A man she hadn't met stood in the living room.

"Sorry to interrupt, but I need to speak with you, Dax."

"Bull, this is Aaron. He's one of the majority shareholders of the Blue Bonnet Mine. You already know Zeke."

Bull shook Aaron's hand, nodding at Zeke, shifting toward Dax. "We have visitors." He opened the front door, motioning outside. "We encountered them riding south."

Dax didn't respond before heading outside. "Running Bear. It's good to see you. Please, come inside. You and your family will join us for supper."

Sliding to the ground, Running Bear walked to within a couple feet of him. "Dax Pelletier. We must talk."

"Of course. We'll speak inside. Swift Bear, Shining Star, and the other woman with you may stay inside with the others."

Giving a brusque nod, Running Bear turned to those with him, explaining what would happen. He motioned for them to follow him inside.

"Billy, I'd like you and Bull to join us for supper. I'd be grateful if you'd keep the others company while

Running Bear and I talk." Dax didn't wait for a response before turning toward his study and closing the door behind him and the Blackfoot chief.

"Please, sit down. May I get you a drink? Coffee with sugar?" Dax knew the older man enjoyed sweetened white man's coffee.

He nodded, an almost imperceptible smile appeared on his face.

Opening the door, Dax spoke with Billy before turning back to Running Bear. "You are well, my friend?"

"I am well. My granddaughter is why I've come to see you."

Thirty minutes later, the men left the study, joining the others in the dining room, Dax's mind reeling from what Running Bear had shared. They'd made an agreement, although Dax didn't believe their decision would be accepted without considerable resistance.

Supper was quiet. Nancy and Aaron stayed silent rather than say anything inappropriate. Running Bear spoke with Dax and Bull as he picked at the food. Rachel had made a traditional American meal, which Swift Bear enjoyed. Shining Star kept her face averted, looking up only when asked a question.

Billy had taken a chair as close to her as Swift Bear would allow. "Your English is quite good, Shining Star."

Her gaze shot to her grandfather, a pleading look in her eyes. "Answer him, Shining Star," Running Bear said in an encouraging voice.

"Thank...you. Grandfather says I must speak the white man words each day."

Billy wanted to ask why she needed to practice English, but decided to stay silent when he met Dax's penetrating gaze. Squirming in his chair, unease speared through him at the occasional odd glances from Running Bear and Dax. Worse, Swift Bear glared at him as if Billy was his enemy.

Sparks of warning tightened his chest, his gut churning, telling him something wasn't right. He wanted to make an excuse, return to the bunkhouse. Something in Dax's severe gaze held him back.

Throat constricting, he swallowed the knot of anxiety growing in his chest. Without doubt, Billy knew whatever was coming would forever alter his life.

Chapter Eighteen

"You want me to do what?" Billy knew the odd glances from Dax, Running Bear, and Swift Bear had been meaningful. Still, he had no idea the ridiculous nature of what they planned. Standing, he paced to the window, running a hand through his unruly hair. At least Shining Star had stayed in the living room with Rachel and the others. She didn't need to be a witness to any of this.

Dax leaned a hip against his desk, arms crossed. "I know this is a lot to take in, Billy."

"I'm not certain what you're asking of me."

"Since the raid that killed Shining Star's brave, the Crow have snuck back at least three times. They almost got away with her twice. The first time, Quiet Wind screamed, warning those in the village. The second, Swift Bear stopped them, injuring one of the Crow. Both times, Shining Star fought as best she could." Dax glanced at Running Bear, who motioned for him to continue.

"The Blackfoot are preparing for their last hunts before the winter weather sets in. Most of the young men will be gone, with only the older men and boys to protect the women. Running Bear is concerned they will not be able to protect Shining Star with Swift Bear gone."

"So they've brought her here to keep her safe. For how long?" Billy asked.

"Until Running Bear believes the danger is over." Standing, Dax returned to his chair, resting his hands on the desk.

Billy massaged the back of his neck. "I don't understand what this has to do with me."

"It's simple. Running Bear has requested you be the one to guard her while she's at the ranch."

"You know that isn't possible, Dax. I have work. We're still breaking horses for the last two Army contracts. There are cattle we need to move to other pastures for the first weeks of winter." He stalked across the room, holding out his hands, palms up. "Why can't she stay with Rachel, Lydia, and Rosemary? The Crow are reckless, but aren't stupid enough to attack Redemption's Edge."

Standing, Running Bear approached Billy, holding his gaze, the older man said nothing for several minutes. By the time he spoke, the only sounds were those of the men breathing.

"This I know, Billy Zales. You care for my granddaughter. You will not allow anyone to harm her. Is this not right?"

He shot nervous glances at Dax and Bull. Blank faces told him he was on his own.

"She is mourning the loss of the man she loved. Shining Star will not want me with her. I mean nothing to your granddaughter."

Running Bear raised a hand. "She is young and does not know what is best for her. You will keep her safe, Billy Zales."

His chest squeezed, throat constricting at the idea of being close to Shining Star every day. After accepting she'd never be a part of his future, Billy wanted to put thoughts of the beautiful woman behind him.

"I'm sorry, but I can't. You'll have to find someone else."

Bull had remained silent, listening and watching Billy's reactions. As his friend, the reasons for Billy's refusal were known to Bull. Standing, he turned toward Running Bear.

"Do you mind if Billy and I speak in private?"

The Blackfoot chief waved his hand. "Go."

"Leave through the side door, Bull." Dax motioned toward a door rarely used, which would take them into the hallway instead of the living room, where everyone waited.

"Come on, Billy." Once in the hall, Bull checked to be sure no one was close by. "There's something else you need to know about Shining Star."

Scrubbing a hand down his face, Billy expelled a frustrated breath. "I don't need to know anything else. I'm not the right person to keep her safe."

Grabbing his shoulders, Bull tightened his hold, voice harsh. "Listen to me. What I have to tell you may change your mind. It may not, but you deserve to know everything." Dropping his hands, he took a step away.

Bull's severe words caught Billy by surprise. "If you believe it's important."

"It is. There's another reason Shining Star is here and needs your protection. The Crow warrior has a reason to take her. It's the same reason the renegades attacked the Blackfoot camp and killed the young man she'd been promised to. She's with child, Billy. The father is the Crow brave."

"I wonder what they're talking about." Rachel shot a furtive glance at Shining Star on the other side of the living room. She'd been in the same position, hands clasped in her lap, head angled downward, since her grandfather, brother, Dax, Bull, and Billy had disappeared into the study, closing the door. Beside her sat the older Blackfoot woman, Quiet Wind, who appeared to act as a chaperone.

"Do you think it involves Shining Star?" Francesca asked, her gaze wandering to where Zeke stood at the front window with Aaron. She knew he was giving her and Nancy time to talk with Rachel before the trip back to Splendor.

"I'm certain of it," Rachel whispered, not wanting Shining Star to feel even more uncomfortable. Standing, she walked to the young Blackfoot woman, kneeling in front of her. "May I get you anything?"

Lifting her face, Shining Star's warm brown eyes met Rachel's bright hazel ones. The young woman's features showed not a hint of the turmoil roiling inside her. Resting her hands over her stomach, she pulled her gaze from Rachel to land on the door to Dax's study.

"Please let me know if you change your mind." Rising, she turned toward the others. "Would anyone like some coffee or more pie?"

Zeke took a few steps away from the window. "The clouds are building. I'm afraid we should get back to town before the storm hits."

"You're welcome to spend the night here. We have extra rooms inside, and two cabins behind the house." Rachel joined him at the window, seeing the rapidly approaching black clouds.

Francesca nodded toward Shining Star. "I believe you may be using them for Running Bear and his people. Zeke is right, we should be going." Hugging Rachel, she stepped aside to let Nancy do the same.

"It was so nice of you to invite us into your home." Aaron offered a small bow. "Please allow me to host you and Dax to supper at the Eagle's Nest when you are in Splendor."

"Thank you, Aaron. You're all welcome here anytime."

Zeke lifted a brow. "Ladies. Are you ready?"

They walked to the front door, Francesca motioning toward the study. "Please give our regards to Dax and the others." She wanted to stay, learn the reason Shining Star appeared so distraught.

"I will. Have a safe journey—" Rachel stopped at the sound of the door behind her opening.

Running Bear walked out first, ignoring everyone as he strode to his granddaughter, who stood as he approached. Staring into her wide eyes, he kept his voice firm and calm.

"It is done."

Bottom lip quivering, tears threatening, Shining Star gave a small nod. "What am I to do?"

In answer, Running Bear turned away, knowing his granddaughter would follow. "We will walk with Billy Zales."

Francesca's hand shook as she brought the cup of tea to her lips. She couldn't quite wrap her mind around the story behind Shining Star's journey to the Pelletier ranch.

Running Bear, Billy, and Shining Star had left the house to talk, the tension between them obvious. While they were gone, Dax and Bull explained the situation, stunning the rest of the visitors. After a brief discussion, and at Rachel's insistence, all the visitors decided to stay the night.

Swift Bear and Quiet Wind sat in a corner, exchanging a few words, but otherwise staying silent. It was clear to everyone how much Swift Bear loved his sister, worried about Shining Star and her future.

It had been decided Shining Star would stay with Bull and his wife, Lydia. A few years earlier, Lydia had been kidnapped and raped by a Crow warrior. At the time, she'd been engaged to Bull. The couple had endured agonizing months, not knowing if their relationship would survive.

"Are you all right?" Zeke lowered himself beside her, covering one of her hands with his.

"I'm fine. I feel so bad about what Shining Star has gone through."

"What surprises me is Running Bear bringing her here."

Francesca's brows drew together. "Why?"

Zeke glanced around, making certain no one else listened. "They prefer to handle tribal issues among themselves."

The front door opened, Running Bear entering, followed by Billy and Shining Star. None of them smiled as they joined the others in the living and dining rooms.

Features showing confusion mixed with resignation, Billy glanced around the room. His entire life had changed in less than twelve hours. Starting tomorrow, he'd be protecting Shining Star.

It was a job he didn't want. A job he couldn't fail.

Francesca and Nancy bounced on the wagon seat the following morning, their thoughts on what they'd witnessed the previous day. Aaron tried several times to start a conversation, each attempt ending in silence.

"I feel so selfish, Nancy. My problems are petty compared to what Shining Star is going through. Zeke believes the reason Running Bear brought her to the Pelletier ranch was because her village wouldn't have accepted a baby that's half Crow. He doubts she'll ever return to her people."

She shot a look at Zeke, who rode a few feet from her side of the wagon, wondering at his thoughts. He'd been unusually quiet since learning of how Billy had been inserted into a situation he played no part in creating. The young man had carried a miserable expression the night before, and when they'd ridden out this morning.

Billy's significant role in protecting Shining Star put a great deal of pressure on a young man who hadn't asked for the responsibility. He'd been tasked with making certain a Crow raiding party didn't swoop down on the ranch and kidnap her. After failing in their attempts at the Blackfoot village, they had a great deal to gain by attacking a ranch owned by wealthy white men.

"It's a terrible situation, Frannie. Shining Star must feel so alone...and scared." Nancy exhaled a slow sigh. "You're right. What she's facing does make our problems appear insignificant. What will her brother do?"

"I'm afraid Swift Bear won't stay. His life is with his people."

They fell into a troubled silence, their gazes focused on the trail toward town. Francesca thought of her and Zeke. Their trip to Redemption's Edge had been enlightening in several ways.

Zeke had been quite attentive, staying close, making it clear he wanted to be with her. She did believe his intentions toward her were honorable. He hoped to make up for the way he'd hurt her by ending their courtship without explanation. Zeke sought a second chance. Even allowing the time they spent together, she still hadn't decided whether or not to grant him one.

Francesca had given up trying to convince herself she didn't love Zeke. She'd fallen for him not long after their first supper together, and through all the turmoil, she had never been able to shove him from her thoughts. By the time their short-lived relationship ended, her heart belonged to the charming lawman.

He hadn't felt the same. At least, that was the impression he'd left when he'd stopped calling on Francesca.

Zeke now told a different story. Francesca had to decide whether or not to believe him. Whether she could risk her heart one more time.

Chapter Nineteen

Wes Acker watched Harmon Tibbs's ranch from a spot a hundred yards from the barn. The one remaining ranch hand sat in a chair on the porch, whittling a small piece of wood, as if waiting for his next orders. Orders which wouldn't be coming from his dead employer.

It wasn't as if the ranch hand didn't know Tibbs had been murdered. With nowhere else to go and animals requiring attention, the older man stayed on, continuing the duties performed prior to the rancher's death.

Wes didn't care about any of this. He'd been ready to ride out of the area, head to Utah, Idaho, or maybe California. It would be easy to get lost in the thousands of people moving to the West Coast state. San Francisco intrigued him, as did the growing town of San Diego.

He'd taken a couple days to consider what was best for him. Stay, and hunt for a stash of money that might not exist, or get out of the territory. Greed won out.

Before leaving, he planned a thorough search of Harmon's house. His gut told him some of the original inheritance had been hidden inside. Maybe as much as another thousand dollars. If Wes was right, the amount he'd retrieve would make the delay in his departure worth it.

Settling his back against a thick tree trunk, he drew a piece of jerky from his saddlebag. The sun wouldn't set for a few more hours, giving him plenty of time to decide his next move.

Hurting or killing the older ranch hand didn't appeal to Wes. Still, he'd do what was necessary to search the house without being seen. No matter what he did or didn't find, he'd be on the trail west within hours, never returning to the Montana Territory.

Gabe slid the wanted poster across the desk toward Zeke. "I asked Sheriff Sterling in Big Pine to check for anyone matching the man we believe killed Harmon and attacked you. He sent this to me. He's wanted for murder."

Zeke studied the drawing, noticing the scar on the left side of his face. The description at the bottom mentioned a Bowie knife, and the suspicion he'd been headed for Montana.

"Wes Acker." Zeke repeated the name, jaw tight as he studied the man's image.

"He's a hired gun. Goes wherever he's offered the most money."

Brows drawing together, Zeke thought of Harmon. "Do you think someone hired him to kill Tibbs?"

Gabe shrugged one shoulder. "I suppose it's possible." Scratching his jaw, he looked down at the wanted poster. "I'm thinking he heard about the money Harmon was carrying and grabbed the opportunity. He might've been in the bank and saw Horace Clausen pass the money to Tibbs."

"I wonder what Harmon planned to do with it. Three thousand is a lot to carry around. Makes the most sense to walk out of the bank and head straight to wherever you planned to use it."

Gabe's lips twisted into an unbelieving sneer. "Where would that be in Splendor? If he was buying property, Clausen would've handled the transfer."

"Cattle? Horses?" Zeke guessed.

"Could've been. He may have planned to take delivery at his ranch. If so, why didn't the sellers come to town when Harmon did show?"

Standing, Zeke walked to the window, staring outside before turning back to Gabe. "He had a ranch hand. I've heard he's still there, taking care of the animals. Maybe he let the sellers know what happened."

Tapping fingers on his desk, Gabe pulled out his pocket watch. "I should take a ride out to Tibbs's ranch and talk to the ranch hand. Probably should take a look around while I'm there."

"I'm going with you."

Chuckling, Gabe stood, grabbing his hat. "Never thought you'd stay behind."

Beauty paced her room, peeking out her window every few minutes in search of one man. Louis Elder had visited Ruby after arriving in Splendor, taking a great deal of time explaining the young woman's guilt in the death of Kyle Forshew. He'd warned her of his intention to take Beauty back to Kansas City to stand trial.

Louis made no threats, using intimidation to make his message clear. Thank goodness few people intimidated Ruby Walsh. Instead of being cowered, the owner of the Palace asked him to leave, suggesting the Dixie or Wild Rose might be more suitable establishments. Once out the door, she'd questioned Beauty before searching out Gabe.

Her timing had been perfect. The sheriff planned to speak with Louis about his reasons for being in Splendor.

Ruby's appearance had allowed him to include the fact a Missouri judge hadn't approved a wanted poster on Beauty. From what Ruby heard, the meeting between the two men hadn't been pleasant.

Louis had grown accustomed to using threats to get his way. He learned they didn't have the same effect on citizens of Splendor as they did in Kansas City.

Careful so no one could see her, Beauty leaned close to the glass, looking up and down the street. She'd hidden away in her room for days, leaving to work downstairs and for no other reason. Sick of living in what amounted to a prison, Beauty gathered her courage.

Grabbing her shawl, she placed a few coins into her reticule before creeping downstairs to a side exit. She couldn't let anyone see her leaving, especially Ruby. For the last few days, she'd been Beauty's gatekeeper.

"Where do you think you're going?"

Beauty stilled with her hand on the doorknob. Turning, she winced at the sight of Ruby, standing with her hands on her hips.

"I'm going crazy in my room. I need to get out for a while."

"Not by yourself. I don't trust that Louis Elder fella. Gabe said he was spitting mad after their meeting. It wouldn't surprise me if he tried to kidnap you and head for Kansas City."

"I don't understand why he'd do that, Ruby. The law isn't looking for me."

Dropping her arms to her sides, her lips twisted. Beauty knew her boss was trying to figure something out.

"Maybe your benefactor's death has nothing to do with why he's here. Is there any other reason he'd come after you?"

Pursing her lips, Beauty thought of what she knew about Louis. "I only met him a few times. Kyle Forshew was his half brother. Same father, different mothers. Their father left Kyle most of his estate, but he did provide Louis with a house and a small income each month. The two never got along well. I never learned why, although Louis was always a little peculiar."

Ruby glanced behind her at the girls trying not to show their interest in the conversation. She waved a hand in the air. "Get on with you, and stop trying to listen to what isn't your business."

Once they dispersed, she turned back to Beauty. "What do you mean about him being peculiar?"

"I don't know." She bit her lower lip, letting out a slow breath. "He asked too many questions, which Kyle ignored most of the time. The worst, though, was Louis would stare at me until my skin began to crawl. It was horrible. And his eyes..." She shook her head, as if ridding herself of a terrible memory. "I'm glad he seldom came around when Kyle and I were together."

The front door opening, and boots pounding on the wood floor, drew their attention. Ruby's face lit up when Deputy Hawke DeBell strode straight toward them. Removing his hat, his gaze shifted between the two women.

"Good afternoon, ladies."

"Hawke, what a nice surprise," Ruby clucked. "Are you here for drinks, or perhaps a little more?"

An odd expression passed over his face, his fingers toying with the brim of his hat. "Just checking on my favorite ladies."

"Such a charmer, Deputy." Ruby blushed enough for Beauty to notice. She'd seen her boss react to few men this way. Hawke DeBell and his fellow deputy, Shane Banderas, were two.

Beauty had never known Hawke to take a woman upstairs. He'd down a couple whiskeys, watch the nightly acts, and flirt with the women, always begging off when receiving an invitation to their room.

There'd been nights she'd studied him from a distance. What she saw wounded her heart. Hawke held a soul deep sorrow within him, a loneliness obvious to others who'd experienced the same. Others such as herself.

"Deputy, you've joined us at the right time. It seems Beauty needs an escort."

Locking his gaze on the reason he frequented the Palace, the woman he'd been drawn to for months, he cleared his throat. "Escort?"

"Has Gabe told you about the threat to Beauty?"

Hawke continued to watch the beautiful, young woman with white-blonde hair and shimmering, silver eyes. "The sheriff let all his deputies know about Louis Elder. Has he approached you, Beauty?"

"I haven't left the Palace since he arrived in town. It's why I need to get outside for a while." She shot a look at Ruby. "Not long, but I'm going crazy in my room."

Hawke saw the opportunity he'd been searching for since first setting eyes on Beauty. "I'd be honored to escort you. Have you eaten?"

"Isn't it a little early for supper, Deputy DeBell?"

He shifted, a smug grin lifting the corners of his mouth. "It depends. Are you hungry, Miss Crawford?"

Eyes widening, she shot a sideways glance at Ruby, who shrugged in response. "How do you know my last name?"

"I know your first name, also. If I'm not mistaken, it's Nellie. Now, are you ready to eat something?"

Beauty felt a surge of unease at Hawke knowing her given name. She'd told no one except Francesca and Horace Clausen when opening her bank accounts. Perhaps sharing a meal with him wouldn't be the worst idea.

"I'm almost always hungry."

"Excellent." Offering his arm, Hawke turned toward Ruby. "Nothing will happen to Beauty while I'm with her."

"Better not, Deputy. She's a special young lady, and I'd be especially angry if Louis gets to her."

"I believe we understand each other, Ruby."

Opening the side door, which exited between the Palace and meat market, Hawke escorted her across the street to the front of McCall's. It was a little early for supper, giving them the choice of several tables. She chose a spot halfway between the front and kitchen.

"Good afternoon, Beauty. Deputy DeBell." Betts lifted the pot of coffee, filling each of their cups. "We have elk meatloaf, roast beef, and chicken fricassee. All come with potatoes and applesauce."

Beauty licked her lips, grimacing when her stomach growled. "I'll have the chicken, please."

"The meatloaf for me, Betts. What's your dessert today?"

The older woman threw back her head and laughed. "I wondered when you'd ask." She looked at Beauty before motioning toward Hawke. "This one sometimes eats dessert first, then eats more after his meal."

Beauty's lips twitched at the small insight into the deputy. "I see no issue with eating dessert twice."

"Neither do I," Hawke said. "So, what do you have for us?"

"Berry pie, orange cake, and cider cake." Betts bent down, lowering her voice. "The cider cake is from yesterday, but still darn good."

Hawke shot a conspiratorial glance at Beauty, who grinned. "I'll have a slice of the cider cake first. How about you, Beauty?"

She thought of the hollow feeling in her stomach, her eyes glistening in mirth. "A small slice would be wonderful, Betts."

"I'll get those to you right away."

Waiting for Betts to walk through the door to the kitchen, Hawke's expression sobered. "If you didn't kill Forshew, and Louis knows it, why travel all this way to confront you?"

Clutching her hands together in her lap, Beauty considered his question. She and Ruby had touched on the same, not settling on an answer.

"Beauty?"

Giving a slow shake of her head, she lifted her gaze to meet his. "I don't know." She repeated what she'd revealed to Ruby about Louis, including his relationship with his half brother.

Hawke rubbed a brow. "There must be a reason he'd travel all this way."

"Here you are." Betts placed a large slice of cake before Hawke, a smaller one in front of Beauty. "I'll bring your meals out in a few minutes."

Picking up his fork, Hawke lifted a large piece toward his mouth, hesitating. "With Forshew dead, who gets his estate?"

"I would assume it would go to Louis."

Chewing slowly, he set down his fork. "What if it didn't pass to Louis?" Pausing a moment, Hawke's jaw tightened. "What if *you* were Forshew's heir?"

Chapter Twenty

Louis couldn't believe his luck. Deciding on an early supper at Eagle's Nest, he'd headed toward the hotel at the same time Beauty appeared with one of the deputies across the street. Moving between two buildings, he watched them step inside McCall's.

Ignoring the sheriff's warning to stay away from her, Louis had continued to search for Beauty. Finding her would change his life, even if it meant ending hers.

Deciding to continue to the St. James instead of being exposed on the boardwalk, he walked the short distance to the hotel. Being there early meant there were a number of empty tables in the dining room. The one next to the window proved perfect, with a clear view of McCall's across the street. He needed to stay vigilant, be ready to follow Beauty and her companion to wherever she lived.

It would be a simple task to arrange her death. Louis had spent a considerable amount of time reviewing various methods of getting rid of her. First, her body had to be found and her death confirmed by someone respected in Splendor. Second, he wanted to avoid too much blood. Third, there could be no evidence leading back to him. And fourth, he required time to return to his room via the back stairs of the hotel.

The concierge, Thomas, would confirm he hadn't seen Louis leave the hotel. Even if the sheriff suspected him, and Gabe would, he'd never be able to prove it.

Eating a meal of consommé, pheasant, potatoes, and fruit compote, he sipped coffee, never taking his attention from McCall's. Satisfaction rolled through him at the thought the obstacle to receiving Kyle's fortune would be eliminated tonight.

Zeke chewed the last bite of beef stew Christina had prepared for him, Hex, and Francesca, who sat next to him. Being careful, he'd taken every chance possible to touch his thigh to hers. He enjoyed the resulting flush, which crept up her neck and face. The surreptitious glances she shot at him were accompanied by the slightest of smiles. She wanted his attention.

"The meal was wonderful, Chrissy. Wish I could stay longer, but Gabe wants to ride out to Tibbs's ranch this evening."

Hex's brows drew together. "What for?"

"We've been talking about the man we believe killed Harmon. We believe his name is Wes Acker, a gun for hire. There's a chance he might go back to the ranch and search the house."

"Hoping to find more money?" Hex asked.

Zeke nodded. "If Acker is the killer, we believe he took the three thousand dollars Harmon withdrew from the bank the same day. He might be arrogant enough to believe no one will stop him from rifling through Harmon's belongings."

Hex pushed his chair back, stretching out his legs. "Isn't there a ranch hand still living there?"

"Gabe heard there is," Zeke answered. "Which means he could be in danger. That's the reason we're riding out tonight."

"I'm going with you."

Zeke wasn't surprised Hex volunteered to ride along. He'd never been one to turn his back on possible danger. "After escorting Frannie home, I need to tack up my horse and meet Gabe at the jail."

"My house is only two doors away, Zeke. I can get there on my own."

"I'm not letting you walk by yourself, Frannie."

Lifting a brow, her piercing glare speared him. "Let me?"

Holding up both hands, he shook his head. "You know that's not what I meant. You're more than capable of walking the short distance home. There's a killer out there somewhere, as well as the man who threatened Beauty. Allow me to escort you home this evening, Frannie."

Refusing to admit Zeke was right, she nodded. "Let me help Chrissy with the dishes."

"I'll help her," Hex said. "You two go on ahead." He looked at Zeke. "I'll meet you at the livery."

"Are you ready, Frannie?" Zeke opened the door. "Thank you again, Chrissy."

"Both of you are welcome anytime."

Zeke draped Frannie's shawl over her shoulders, offering comfort from the cool evening air. October ushered in the first signs of winter, the temperatures dropping more each day. By November, they'd have the season's initial snow.

"Are you warm enough?" He didn't wait for an answer before draping his arm over her shoulders.

Instead of pulling away, she leaned into him. "I'm fine...now."

Her words tugged at his heart, desire sending spirals of heat through him. Zeke didn't want to assume too much from her response. He still had a ways to go to get her to trust him again, believe he wouldn't walk away a second time. For now, he would accept whatever time together she'd allow.

Reaching her front door, the sound of laughter came from inside. "Nancy cooked supper for Aaron. She's been spending some time with Suzanne Barnett at the boardinghouse restaurant, learning a few recipes." Frannie's mouth twisted into a grin. "It's an experiment, as she never learned to cook while growing up."

"At least there are two voices coming from inside, which means she didn't poison him."

Trying to stifle a laugh, she leaned into Zeke. "Not yet. I suppose it could still happen."

One brow lifting, he leaned to the side enough to look through the window. "She's serving dessert."

"Maybe I should go inside and taste it before anything happens to Aaron."

Turning to face her, he settled his hands on her waist, drawing her close. "My dessert isn't inside. It's right here." Leaning down, slow enough for her to step away, he covered her mouth with his.

Feeling her hands creep up his arms to wrap around his neck, Zeke continued his gentle assault on her mouth. Nipping at the edges, his tongue traced the plump fullness of her lips, eliciting a guttural moan from deep in her throat. Hands splaying across her back, he closed the tiny distance between them, aligning her body with his as he continued to plunder her mouth.

Strings of fire flashed through him at her soft groans of pleasure. She was enjoying this as much as him. He knew it couldn't go on. Understood they had to stop. Doing so took longer than it should've. A long minute later, he broke the kiss, lifting his face to rest his forehead against hers.

Keeping his hands on her waist, his body began to react to the rise and fall of her chest against his. Zeke fought to find his breath. Struggled to force himself to step away.

Putting almost a foot between them, he bent again, brushing an almost chaste kiss over her lips. "Are you all right, Frannie?"

Lifting her hand, she touched fingers to her mouth, not bothering to hide a grin. "I'm very much all right, Zeke. Perhaps we can do that again sometime." The instant the words were out, she felt her face heat. "What I mean is—"

He silenced her with one more, brief kiss. "As often as you'll allow me, Frannie." Reaching for the doorknob, he opened it a crack. "I should meet Hex at the livery. May I call on you for supper tomorrow?"

"Yes, you may." Lifting onto her toes, she kissed his cheek. "Please be careful tonight."

"Always." Turning, Zeke walked straight down the street toward the livery.

Moving to the edge of the porch, Francesca leaned against a post, a ragged sigh escaping. She'd promised herself to take her time with Zeke, protect her heart as she hadn't done before. Each time they were together, her resolve cracked a little more, the desire she felt increasing.

Francesca thought of the secret she'd shared with no one. Not even Nancy, her closest friend, and a woman she confided in about everything.

If her relationship with Zeke continued to grow, there'd come a time she'd have to tell him the truth. The thought caused a frisson of fear.

Once learning of her secret, most men would turn her away. Francesca gripped the post tighter, telling hersellf Zeke wasn't *most men*. She then recalled how wrong she'd been about him when they'd first courted.

Stiffening at the sound of the front door opening, she forced herself to turn away from the street. "Good evening, Aaron." She glanced behind him, not seeing Nancy. "Should I ask about supper?"

A smile broke across his face. "Nancy made a wonderful chicken stew. I told her not to try anything fancy. The stew was perfect."

Francesca took a step closer, lowering her voice. "You like her, don't you?"

Glancing over his shoulder, Aaron matched the volume of his voice to hers. "Very much. Do you think she might have an interest in me?"

Reaching out, she patted his arm. "I believe Nancy has a great deal of interest in you."

"That's, well...that's wonderful." His face relaxed with the knowledge. "Yes, quite wonderful. Thank you, Frannie. Well, it's time I continued home."

On a whim, she called after him. "Will you live in Splendor or return to New York?"

Stopping, he turned around, his expression turning somber. "Wherever Nancy wants, of course."

Francesca watched him walk toward the house he rented from Noah, the lightness in his step causing her to smile. Nancy deserved love, and Aaron might be the perfect man to provide it.

Entering the house, she walked straight into the bedroom the women shared, hoping her best friend wasn't too tired to talk. Sitting at the vanity, Nancy drew a brush through her long hair, humming under her breath. Setting down the brush, she shifted to look at Francesca.

"How was supper with Hex and Chrissy?"

"Quite nice. Zeke was there." Francesca sat down in a chair near the window, tucking her legs under her. "I was outside when Aaron left. He said your supper was wonderful."

Nancy beamed at his compliment. "He told me the same. I do hope he meant it."

Grabbing a nearby quilt, she placed it over her legs. "I'm certain he did."

"He's coming for supper again tomorrow. Unless you have plans to cook for Zeke."

"I'm not certain what we're doing for supper. Please go ahead with your plans." Francesca picked at the fabric of the quilt, nervous about what she wanted to reveal. "Do you have a few minutes to talk?"

Moving to the bed, Nancy sat down, resting her back against the headboard. "I have as much time as you want, Frannie."

Nodding, she inhaled a slow breath, letting it out in a ragged stream. "This isn't easy for me to talk about."

"All right."

"It has to do with Edmund...and me. I haven't spoken to anyone else about it." Rubbing her hands along the quilt, she glanced at Nancy, then looked away. "I was pregnant when Edmund ended our engagement."

Sitting up, Nancy moved to the edge of the bed. "Pregnant? Did that worthless man know?"

She gave a slow shake of her head. "No. I suspected, but didn't know myself until a couple weeks later. It wouldn't have mattered. I never would've married a man who didn't want me."

Nancy watched her, remaining silent about what Francesca hadn't said.

"I was almost four months along when I lost the baby."

Jumping from the bed, Nancy knelt in front of her, taking her hands in hers. "I'm so sorry, Frannie. I wish you would've told me. I could've been there for you."

Swiping a lone tear rolling down her cheek, she pulled her hands free, gripping the edges of the quilt. "It happened during an appointment at the clinic. Even though it wasn't the one my family used, I made the doctor and nurses promise to say nothing to my family. I was fortunate they were all females."

Nancy moved to a nearby settee. "A female doctor. How wonderful."

Choking out a broken laugh, Francesca nodded. "Yes, it was. She had me return to make certain there were no complications. My family never knew, of course. I went home, telling Mother I wasn't feeling well. After a couple days, I returned to the law office."

"And continued on as if nothing happened," Nancy added.

"Yes. Then I received the letter from Rachel Pelletier. The timing was perfect."

Nancy studied her, guessing the real reason for Francesca revealing her secret. "Zeke doesn't know, does he?"

Swallowing a tight ball of fear, she licked her lips, staring at her clasped hands. "No."

"Zeke is a good man who cares a great deal about you. It won't matter to him, Frannie."

"How do you know?"

"Because men out here are different from the ones back east. They're stronger, willing to accept challenges that would cause those on the Northeast Coast to run. Unlike most of the men we grew up with, many of the ones out here fought in the war, sacrificed a great deal before traveling west for a new life. Zeke is one of those men."

Francesca let Nancy's words roll around in her head. They made a great deal of sense, and did describe Zeke. He was a good, strong man. She just prayed he was also one who'd forgive the mistakes in her past.

Chapter Twenty-One

"Where you boys headed tonight?" Hawke sat at Gabe's desk, his boots propped on top, hands linked together over his stomach.

Zeke grabbed a chair, whipping it around to straddle it. "Hex and I are riding out to Harmon Tibbs's ranch with Gabe. He wants to make certain the man who killed him isn't hiding out there."

"I heard the ranch hand is still there." Dropping his boots to the floor, Hawke rested his hands on the desk. "Older man, from what I recall."

Hex crossed his arms, leaning against a wall. "I heard the same. Another reason to ride out. Make sure the man is all right out there by himself."

The door swung open, Gabe entering. "Are you ready, Zeke?"

Standing, he set the chair aside. "I'm ready. Hex is riding with us."

Giving a crisp nod, Gabe looked at Hawke. "I heard you had supper with Beauty."

"Small town gossip." Shoving from the desk, he walked around it to lean a hip against the edge. "Beauty's been stuck inside the Palace because of Louis Elder. She wanted to get out for a couple hours, but Ruby refused to let her go alone." Hawke lifted one shoulder in a shrug. "I escorted her back about thirty minutes ago."

"She's a nice lady stuck in a bad situation."

The three men turned their attention toward Zeke. "You know her?" Hawke asked.

"Met her at the Palace. If you're asking if I know her better than that, the answer is no."

Gabe closed the distance to the door. "Enough of this, gentlemen. We need to get going."

Outside, Zeke scanned the street, an odd sensation niggling.

"Something wrong?" Hex swung into his saddle.

Mouth twisting into a grimace, Zeke mounted his horse. "An odd feeling we're being watched. Nothing specific, and I don't see anyone. Still..." His voice trailed off as he glanced around one more time.

"Let's go." Gabe rode south from the jail, reining east when they reached the edge of town.

They hadn't gone far, less than half a mile, when an explosion rocked the ground, the sound echoing around them. Reining around, the three watched in horror at the sight of flames rising from the center of town.

Louis watched flames engulf Ruby's Palace from the third floor window of his room at the St. James. A smug grin tugged at the corners of his mouth. Beauty couldn't have escaped the explosion or resulting fire.

Leaning back in his chair, he lifted the glass of brandy to his lips, taking a satisfying swallow. With her death, Kyle's estate would now pass to Louis.

The hasty plan had been brilliant. While waiting for Beauty and the deputy to leave McCall's, Louis had returned to his room, grabbing his gun and stuffing dynamite into a pocket. Leaving out the back door, he'd hidden between the hotel and Emporium, resuming his vigil of McCall's. It wasn't long before the two emerged.

Following at a safe distance, Louis wasn't surprised when they entered the Palace. It shouldn't have surprised him that a former mistress would find employment in what amounted to an upscale brothel. Ruby might advertise music and entertainment, but everyone in town knew what services the women offered.

Waiting until the deputy left, Louis watched, seeing a light brighten a second floor room. Running to the back, he placed both sticks of dynamite at the corner below Beauty's room. The darkness hid his movements. Taking a quick look around, he lit the fuses and ran.

He'd reached Frontier Street when the explosion occurred. The ground, buildings, and air around him shuddered from the blast. Slowing his pace, Louis continued to the back entrance of the hotel, returning to his room.

Taking another sip of brandy, he wondered if anyone survived the blast. Chuckling, he realized how little he cared. He wanted the money, which should've gone to him. The means to obtain it wouldn't cause even a second of lost sleep.

Watching townsfolk run around with buckets of water and shovels, he considered joining them. Acting as a good citizen could help him defray suspicion away from him.

Instead of rushing downstairs, he refilled his glass with brandy. Louis had never been one to volunteer. Definitely not if it included working with his hands while getting his tailored clothes dirty.

Three riders appeared from the south, dismounting by the jail before running between buildings toward the Palace. He recognized Sheriff Evans, but not the other two.

Finishing his brandy, Louis decided it was time to survey the destruction, confirm Beauty hadn't found a way out. Taking his time, he left the hotel through the front entrance, making certain to acknowledge Thomas on his way out.

Chaos reigned in the area around the Palace. Noah Brandt stood near a fire engine, barking orders to the volunteers. Sheriff Evans, sleeves rolled up, directed people with buckets of water, and those shoveling dirt onto the flames.

Louis stood aside and watched, surprised at their progress. He'd underestimated the town's ability to work together. Judging by the damage to the Palace, their progress didn't matter. Most of the back of the building had disappeared, the rest of the structure engulfed in flames.

"No one could've survived," he muttered to himself, ready to turn away when a hand landed on his shoulder.

Hawke spun him around, his hard glare boring into Louis's. "Sheriff Evans will want to talk to you about what happened here. You're going to wait in the jail until he's finished."

"Jail? Me? Why would you do that?" Louis tried to release the deputy's hold without success.

"You're the only person in town who wished Beauty harm. That's all the reason needed to arrest you."

Eyes wide with indignation, Louis shook his head. "You can't arrest me for something I didn't do."

"Maybe you did, maybe not. We'll worry about that later." Tightening his grip, Hawke hauled Louis to the jail, locking him in one of the cells. "Someone will check on you later."

Grasping the bars, Louis yelled after him. "You can't do this. I'll have your badge for this."

Without stopping, Hawke glanced over his shoulder. "You can try."

"Wait!"

"What now, Louis?"

"Did everyone make it out of the building?"

Anger roared through Hawke. His gut told him this man was responsible for the destruction, and possible deaths. "You better pray they did."

Three hours later, Zeke held Francesca's hand, both covered in dirt and soot as they surveyed the scene. A few feet away, Aaron and Nancy stood together, also holding hands. The grim features on all four expressed their thoughts.

By the grace of God, no one had died. Everyone except Beauty had been downstairs. The instant the blast sounded, they ran out the front door and down the street.

Hawke had arrived within minutes of the explosion, finding Beauty in a ball just inside the side door. Scooping her into his arms, he'd run to the clinic, which had suffered the effects of the blast. Located behind the Palace, the front windows were broken, shards of glass covering the street.

Doctors McCord and Worthington had arrived at the same time Hawke kicked in the front door, laying Beauty on one of the examination beds. Obtaining assurances from both doctors she'd be all right, he'd joined the others outside, continuing to fight the blaze until only embers remained.

Francesca looked up at Zeke "What will Ruby do now?"

Tightening his hold on her hand, he stared at the carnage. "Rebuild. The town will help, the same as we did after the fire in Chinatown. Same with repairing the clinic. We're fortunate no other buildings were damaged."

Zeke stroked a hand down her hair. "It's close to midnight. You should get some sleep. I'll walk you home."

They moved on tired legs, bodies aching from carrying buckets of water and shoveling dirt. The fire engine Noah brought to town a year earlier helped a great deal, cutting down the time to douse the fire by half.

Knowing Aaron and Nancy were several yards behind them, Zeke brushed a kiss across her cheek, not lingering as he wanted. "There will be a lot of clean-up the next couple days, Frannie. I don't know when I'll be free to see you."

"I plan to help Suzanne make and deliver meals for those helping." A warm smile tugged at her lips. "I'm certain we'll see each other." Going up on her toes, she kissed his cheek. "Sleep well, Zeke."

He wanted to stay, kiss her senseless, as he'd done earlier that evening. Before doing something he shouldn't, Zeke touched the brim of his hat and left.

Gabe caught his attention, motioning him toward a group of deputies standing at the back of the general store. Joining them, he listened to a conversation he hadn't expected this soon after the explosion.

Hawke shoved his hat back from his forehead. "Someone should go through his room tonight, Gabe. We aren't going to be able to hold him at the jail for long."

"You're right." Gabe glanced around the group of men, all exhausted, clothes streaked with a combination of smoke, soot, and dirt. "I want two of you, who have no connection to Beauty, to search Elder's room. Caleb and

Mack." The two close friends lifted tired eyes to their boss. "I know you have children at home, but this shouldn't take long."

"We'll head right over, Gabe," Caleb answered. "Anything in particular we're looking for?"

"Dynamite," Hawke said.

Gabe nodded at the quick response. "Plus documents of any kind that could prove he came out here to harm Beauty. Her real name is Nellie Crawford. Also, her benefactor in Kansas City was businessman Kyle Forshew. He was also Elder's half brother."

Zeke stepped forward. "There's a chance Forshew may have left his estate to Beauty."

Cash Coulter chuckled, tugging on his mustache. "That could be the reason for wanting Beauty dead."

"I can keep him at the jail overnight."

"We won't need more than an hour, Gabe," Mack said. "We'll be back at the jail with anything we find."

"Good. We'll be helping to clean up the mess tomorrow morning. The rest of you head home and get some sleep. The next few days are going to be long."

"I'll be at the clinic, Gabe." Hawke didn't wait for anyone to argue with him. Not that he expected them to.

He'd been the one to escort Beauty to supper and back to the Palace. Thirty minutes later, the place had blown up, and he'd been the one to miss whoever had followed them. If he was right, that person was already behind bars.

Hawke hoped Caleb and Mack would find enough evidence to keep Louis Elder there for life.

Chapter Twenty-Two

Francesca moaned, the feel of Zeke's hands moving over her back causing tendrils of heat to whip through her. She'd never felt anything so wonderful, making her want to lose all control, give into the sensual pleasure of his touch.

Reaching out, she searched him out. Instead of the hard plains of his chest, or sculptured muscles of his arms, her hand landed on something smooth and cold. Eyes popping open, she groaned. The empty bed underscored the truth. It was a dream, one of many she'd been having about the man who controlled most of her waking thoughts.

"You're awake." Nancy walked in, a cup of coffee in one hand. Swallowing a sip, she pushed open the curtains, her gaze taking in the lingering smoke from last night's explosion. Lowering herself onto the settee, she lifted the cup again. "Would you like some?"

Sitting up, Francesca rubbed her eyes, still feeling the ghost-like touch of Zeke's hands. "Not yet. What time is it?"

"Almost ten."

"Ten?" She slid to the ground, hurrying to take care of her personal needs and dress. "I promised Suzanne I'd help prepare food for the people cleaning up after the blast."

"Don't fret, Frannie. I went over early to help with breakfast and deliver coffee. Suzanne knows you had a long night." Nancy's calm didn't quite make its way to Francesca.

Grabbing her shawl and oversized hat, she walked toward the front. "Everyone was up late last night. I never stay in bed this long. Have you heard anything about Beauty?"

"Suzanne heard from Olivia McCord that Beauty is doing much better. If she continues to improve, Doc McCord will allow her to leave the clinic tomorrow."

Following her, Nancy set her empty cup on the table, picking up her bonnet and wrap. "Are you ready?"

"Yes. I hope we're in time to help prepare lunch." Francesca opened the front door, letting out a yelp when she almost walked into Zeke. Seeing her wobble, he reached out, gripping her shoulders.

Staring down into her eyes, he loosened his hold. "Are you all right?"

"You startled me. I should've been more aware."

"You appear to be in a hurry." Dropping his hands, he stepped away.

His dirt covered clothes and haggard expression finally registered on her. "You're exhausted. Come inside. Nancy made coffee."

Zeke glanced down at himself, chuckling. "I look much worse than I am, Frannie. We've made a great deal of progress. Most of the ruined material has been cleared away. Noah and Silas Jenks, at the lumber mill, are meeting with Ruby about rebuilding.”

“How is Ruby doing?”

Massaging the back of his neck, Zeke shrugged. “Better than you’d expect. She’s a strong woman, and mad as a wet cat about what happened. Ruby is certain Louis Elder set the dynamite.”

“I believe the same.”

“So do I.” Nancy joined them on the front porch, closing the door behind her. “This morning, Suzanne Barnett told me Hawke arrested him. Is it true, Zeke?”

Placing a hand at each of their backs, he guided them down the stairs and toward the boardinghouse. “Yes. Caleb and Mack searched his room for two hours, but found nothing tying him to the blast. Gabe is going to have to let him go.”

“There must be some type of evidence against him.” Francesca bit her lower lip, brows drawn together. “He came here for Beauty. Doesn’t it seem too much of a coincidence her place of work is destroyed within days of his arrival?”

“A coincidence it is *not*.” Nancy stopped at the charred remains of the Palace, placing a hand over her roiling stomach. “It’s so distressing. I’m afraid if Louis is set free, he’ll go after the poor girl again until he kills her. Where will she stay when Doc McCord allows her to leave?”

Zeke stood between the two women, surveying the remains of the Palace. “Noah is preparing three of his empty houses for Ruby's ladies and bartenders. She'll be staying at the St. James."

"And Beauty?" Francesca asked.

"Nick mentioned Suzanne has prepared a room for her at the boardinghouse. Once she is healed, she'll share space in one of the houses with the other ladies until the Palace is rebuilt. I'll escort the two of you to Suzanne's, unless there's somewhere else you intend to go."

Francesca glanced up at Zeke. "If you're needed here, we're perfectly capable of walking the rest of the way."

"Oh. There's Aaron." Nancy hurried away before the other two could respond.

"I'm afraid she's smitten with Aaron."

Zeke's gaze moved over Francesca's face, warmth spreading through him. He knew he was much more than smitten with the woman beside him.

"I believe Aaron feels the same," she continued, unaware of Zeke's close scrutiny. Turning her attention toward him, she raised her head, breath catching at the blatant look of desire on his face. "Zeke?"

Taking her hand, he walked behind the clinic, continuing to his house a few buildings away. Throwing the door open, he tugged her inside. Before losing his courage, Zeke turned her to face him, lowering his mouth to hers.

Francesca's arms wrapped around his neck as the kiss deepened, the gentle assault turning ardent and hungry. Pulse racing, a moan escaped when his lips trailed down her neck, then back up to claim her mouth once more.

Minutes passed before he raised his head, breath coming in gasps. He could feel her heart pounding against his chest, a beat in rhythm with his own. Gazing into her eyes, he parted his lips when she lifted a finger to trace a path along his sensual mouth.

"Frannie…" It was a plea…a prayer…a hope for more. Leaning down, he pressed a kiss to the tip of her nose. "I want you, Frannie."

"I want you, too."

"But not like this."

Giving a slow shake of her head, she pressed her lips together. "No. Not like this."

Straightening, he looked out the front window of his house. "Suzanne needs your help, and Gabe expects me at the jail. We should go." His hands continued to splay across her lower back, fingers massaging in a light caress through the fabric of her dress.

"Yes," she breathed out, not moving from her place within his embrace.

"Once more, Frannie." Leaning down, he brushed another kiss over her already sensitive mouth, delving inside for the briefest of moments before lifting his head.

Releasing his grip, Zeke reached out, threading his fingers through hers. "Will this embarrass you?"

A wicked grin tipped up the corners of her mouth. "I doubt there's much you could do that would embarrass me. Anger me, perhaps, but not cause embarrassment."

Chuckling, he opened the door, tugging her outside. "I don't know how long I'll be, but I want to see you again...today." Tightening his grip on her hand, he retraced their steps to what was left of the Palace.

"Would you be available to come for supper tonight?"

"I would." Zeke didn't stop walking until they arrived at the boardinghouse. "I'd kiss you again, but it wouldn't be wise." Lifting their joined hands, he brushed his lips over her knuckles. "I'll see you this evening."

"Yes, you will." She disappeared inside, staring out a window until he walked out of sight. Francesca knew what she and Zeke had was right. More than she'd ever dreamed of having.

Turning from the window, a sharp pain almost doubled her over. Placing a hand on her stomach, she bent over, sucking in air. Experiencing a brief moment of panic, Francesca glanced around, relieved to realize all the women were working in the kitchen.

Tears stinging her eyes, she didn't have to guess to know what triggered the pain. Her instincts told her it wouldn't be long before Zeke proposed. The thought thrilled and alarmed her.

The time had come to explain her past, confess what she'd revealed to just one other person. Francesca knew it would take all her courage to face him, and an uncommon understanding from the man who held their future in his hands.

"You can't keep me in jail. I demand to be released." Louis Elder grasped the bars with both hands, his face a blotchy red from hours of yelling his ultimatums.

Deputy Beth Evans, Chan Evans' wife, walked toward the cell, stopping a few feet away. "Sheriff Evans isn't in the jail. He's the only one with the authority to let you out, Mr. Elder. I'd suggest you sit down and stay calm until he returns."

"Stay calm? I've been behind these bars since last night with no idea why." Huffing out frustrated breaths, he glared at Beth. "I want a lawyer."

"Do you have one in Splendor?"

"Miss Francesca O'Reilly. Someone needs to alert her of my situation."

Beth's brow lifted at the familiar name. "Are you certain you retained Miss O'Reilly?"

"Of course I'm certain. Send someone for her." There was no mistaking the authority in his words. It didn't mean she couldn't ignore the command.

"You can request we speak to Miss O'Reilly once the sheriff returns, Mr. Elder."

"Beth. Are you here?"

Her shoulders relaxed at her husband's voice. "In the back, Chan."

A U.S. Marshal, Chan Evans was often out of town, moving convicted criminals from Big Pine to the territorial prison near Deer Lodge, or wherever the judge directed. The job would've been easier if they'd moved to Big Pine, but Sheriff Parker Sterling didn't have an opening for a deputy. Beth wasn't ready to focus solely on cooking, gardening, and laundry. As a former federal agent, she still required the excitement of hunting and bringing in criminals. At least until they were ready to have children.

"You there."

Chan's head whirled toward Louis. "Is there something I can do for you?"

"I've requested someone go after my lawyer. This...*woman*...has refused to fetch her. You need to get her for me."

"As I told you, Sheriff Evans must approve one of us requesting she come to the jail." Irritation laced her explanation. "As you can see, he isn't here. I'll speak with him as soon as he arrives."

The sound of the front door opening, boots thudding on the wood floor, drew their attention. Gabe walked around the corner, a grin forming at the sight of his brother.

"Is there a meeting I missed?"

"I demand someone get my lawyer."

Gabe turned to face their prisoner, the humor in his voice gone. "You have a lawyer in Splendor?"

"Francesca O'Reilly. I want to see her...now!"

Without answering, Gabe motioned for Beth and Chan to follow him to the front. The action set off another round of shouting from Louis.

"Has he been this way all day?"

Beth blew out a frustrated breath. "All day, Gabe. If you approve, I'll see if Frannie is in her office."

"Go ahead. If she isn't in her office, leave a message on her desk."

"Be right back."

Once the door closed, Gabe sat down, tapping fingers on the arm of his chair. "We're missing something. All my instincts tell me Elder blew up the Palace, but Caleb and Mack found nothing in his hotel room."

Chan lifted his boots, setting them on the desk, ignoring Gabe's disgusted glare. "Then you're looking in the wrong place."

"He just arrived a few days ago. If not his room, where else could he hide evidence?"

Stroking the scruff on his chin and jaw, Chan's eyes narrowed. "It's got to be someplace where no one can stumble across it. Someplace secure." A moment later, his features brightened. "Have you spoken to Horace Clausen?"

Gabe's mouth twisted in bewilderment. "The bank manager? Why?"

Setting his boots on the floor, Chan leaned forward. "Because Clausen installed those new-fangled boxes to keep belongings safe about a year ago."

Pointing a finger at his youngest brother, Gabe smiled. "*You* are a genius."

"Well, dang, I've been telling you that for years."

Chapter Twenty-Three

"Are you certain Louis Elder told you he'd retained me to represent him, Beth?" Francesca's voice and expression were incredulous.

"He insisted you're his attorney. Chan and Gabe also heard him."

Shaking her head, Francesca glanced at Nancy leaning against the bookcase a few feet away. "The man is delusional. I did meet with him, but did not accept him as a client. Besides not believing anything the man told me, I'm already representing Nellie Crawford."

"Beauty?" Beth asked. "Does he know she's your client?"

"No, and it's none of his business. He'll need to find someone else."

Beth's lips twisted. "I don't recall there being another attorney in Splendor."

"There isn't." Francesca reached into a drawer, pulling out a piece of paper. Jotting down a name, she handed it to Beth. "I have no idea how good he is. At least it's a name."

Nancy moved away from the bookcase, plucking the paper from Beth's hand. "You are not going to help Louis Elder in any way. After all, it is almost certain he's the man who tried to kill Beauty."

"Innocent until proven guilty," Francesca admonished, unable to hide a small smile.

Crossing her arms, Nancy's jaw clenched. "The sheriff will find the proof to convict him. I'm certain of it."

"I hope you're right. Elder is one of the most obnoxious men I've ever had the displeasure of knowing." Beth paced a few feet away, whipping around to lock a questioning gaze on Francesca. "Are you and Zeke together?"

Jaw dropping, the same as the pen in her hand, Francesca stuttered. "Well...um..."

"Yes, they are. The same as Aaron and me. And close your mouth, Frannie. You look ridiculous."

Mouth twitching, Beth couldn't quite stop a chuckle. "Well, I'm happy for both of you. I've only met Aaron Haas, so know little about him. Without doubt, Zeke is one of the best men I know." Stopping, as if considering her next words, she rested her hands on the back of a large guest chair. "This may sound strange, given how confident he appears, but I do believe he sometimes struggles with the change in his fortune."

Francesca rested her arms on the desk. "Fortune?"

"You may not know, but the Boudreaux family was quite wealthy. In fact, Josephine Lucero learned they were quite high in the social circles of New York. She's from New Orleans, and knew of the Boudreaux family. After Hex and Zeke left to join the Confederate cause, their father had a complete breakdown. He lost their entire fortune. Hex and Zeke tried to revive the business when they returned, but it wasn't possible. Zeke took it quite hard."

Francesca thought of the conversation she had with him, his reservations about their courtship. She cared nothing about the lack of wealth. She'd fallen in love with the man he'd become. Resilient, honest, and hardworking.

"He's come through all of it well. I've yet to meet anyone who doesn't respect him." Francesca knew she sounded defensive, protective of the man she hoped to have in her future.

Beth grinned, pleased with her friend's answer. "I should get back to the jail. Elder won't be happy with what I have to tell him." Her grin widened, signaling how little she cared.

When Beth closed the door, Nancy sat down across from Francesca. "What if they don't find evidence proving Louis tried to kill Beauty?"

"I don't know. Perhaps he'll give up and return to Kansas City."

"You don't believe that, do you, Frannie?"

"No. If Gabe has to let him go, Louis will try again."

"Why does he hate her so much?"

"I don't believe he does, Nancy. There's another reason he wants her dead."

A crisp rap on the door had Nancy rushing to open it. "Mr. Griggs."

Waving a telegram in the air, Bernie took a step into the office. "This came for you, Miss O'Reilly. It's from Kansas City."

Walking around the desk, she took the telegram from Bernie's hand and read it. A small smile tipped the edges of her mouth. Lifting her gaze to the short, wiry man, she saw the almost imperceptible acknowledgment on his face. Bernie knew more personal information on the townsfolk than anyone else. Thank goodness he never whispered a word to anyone. Secrets were always safe with him.

"Good news?" Nancy clasped her hands in front of her, mouth drawn into a thin line, finding it hard to contain her curiosity.

"Thank you, Bernie. I appreciate you bringing it to me."

Bouncing on the balls of his feet, he waved off her thanks. "Knew it was important. Besides, I needed to get out of the office for a few minutes." Chuckling, he left, his footfalls echoing down the stairs.

"What does it say, Frannie?"

"It's from the attorney Kyle Forshew used in Kansas City. He confirmed the Forshew estate wasn't left to Kyle's half brother, Louis." Eyes glistening, she lifted the telegram. "The entire estate was left to Nellie Crawford."

"This is quite an unusual request, Sheriff." Horace Clausen motioned for Gabe to follow him. Opening a door to a small room, he checked numbers on each of the metal boxes secured against one wall. Stopping, he checked the numbers before inserting a key into a door and opening it. Reaching inside, he pulled out a separate metal box. "Here you are. If you don't mind, and since you are not the owner, I'll stay."

"Fine with me, Horace." Taking the box, he set it on a counter against another wall. Lifting the lid, Gabe took out a lone piece of paper. Reviewing the contents, he handed the page to Horace. "What do you think?"

Reading it, the banker set the paper back into the box. "That would seem to be a solid motive."

Gabe closed the lid. "An excellent motive for wanting Beauty dead."

Leaving the bank, he walked next door, opening the door to Francesca's office. Stepping inside, he heard voices from upstairs before seeing Francesca and Nancy come into view.

"Sheriff. We were coming to speak with you." Joining him by the front door, Francesca held up the telegram. "I received this reply to a message sent to Kyle Forshew's lawyer in Kansas City." Handing him the telegram, they waited while he read through it.

"This confirms what I learned from Horace Clausen."

Francesca inched closer. "What do you mean?"

"It's why I wanted to speak with you." Explaining the contents of the security box at the bank, he handed the telegram back to her. "Keep this safe. We will need it and Forshew's last instructions when Elder goes to trial."

"With him locked inside the jail, do you believe Beauty's still in danger?"

"I can't say for certain, Frannie." Gabe rubbed his jaw. "Have you seen anyone else in town who might be working with Elder?"

"No one." She shot a look at Nancy, who continued her silence. "Were there provisions in his will for what would happen if both Beauty and Louis are dead? Another beneficiary?"

"I'm no expert, but I didn't notice anything, Frannie. There was just one piece of paper. If you're interested, Horace will allow you to see what's there."

"If you've verified Louis Elder is the beneficiary if Beauty is dead, I'm satisfied." Again, she held up the telegram. "Plus we have the statement from the attorney, which confirms what you saw."

"Chan wants to move Elder to Big Pine for trial. He already sent a telegram to Judge Collins for approval."

"An excellent idea. There is at least one good attorney in Big Pine who can represent him."

"Will you act as the prosecutor?" Gabe asked.

"I will, unless Beauty hires someone else. Montana doesn't have public prosecutors, so she'll have to retain someone."

Nancy spoke for the first time. "You're the best choice, Frannie. When you're done with Elder, he'll spend the rest of his life in prison."

Zeke stood behind Francesca, resting his hands on her waist while watching her prepare their supper. Brushing a kiss below her ear, he felt her shiver.

"You're distracting me."

"I'd hope so." He continued to nibble down her neck, hearing her soft moan.

"If you continue, I could end up ruining our supper."

"You have your job, Frannie, and I have mine."

She leaned back against him, continuing to stir the chicken stew. "And it's to distract me."

Moving his mouth to her ear, his voice grew husky. "Just letting you know I'm here, darlin'."

Wanting him to continue, she turned in his arms. "Believe me, Zeke, I know you're here."

Lowering his head, he brushed a kiss across her lips before settling his mouth over hers.

Francesca loved the feel of his body against hers, his warm mouth creating a magical effect on all her most intimate places. The lightest touch would cause spirals of heat to flash through her, his voice creating shivers of need. A sudden sense of unease caused her to break the kiss and step away.

"We should eat before the stew cooks too long."

Letting his hands skim along her arms, he dropped them to his sides, a small smile aimed at her. "How can I help?"

She glanced at the table, satisfied the plates, flatware, and napkins were in place. "Would you pour coffee for us?"

Opening the cupboard, he removed two cups and filled them from the pot on the stove. Setting them on the table, he found himself watching Francesca.

She'd been tense since he'd arrived almost an hour earlier. They'd talked about what Gabe found at the bank and the telegram from Forshew's attorney. Once those subjects had been exhausted, Francesca fell silent, concentrating on their meal. A rare occurrence for a woman who had an opinion on everything.

"Do you mind if I put the stew pot on the table?" Her voice shook a little, another sign something bothered her.

"Doesn't matter to me where you put it." When she set it down, he came up behind her, placing his hands on her shoulders. "What's wrong, Frannie?"

"Wrong?"

"You're acting like a skittish colt. Something's bothering you, and I want to know what it is."

Moving out of his grasp, she set aside the towels used to move the pot over. "Let's eat first, then we'll talk."

Walking to the counter, Zeke picked up a lid, setting it on top of the stew pot. "We'll talk first."

Lips thinning, her back stiffened. "You may not be hungry after I say what's needed."

Jaw tight, his voice held an edge not there when he arrived. "I'll take that chance, Frannie."

Resigned, she motioned to the living room. "Let's at least be comfortable." Taking a seat at one end of the sofa, he sat on the other end, placing his arm along the back.

"All right. Tell me what has you so upset."

Chapter Twenty-Four

Francesca told herself Zeke would be reasonable, listen to her, and ask questions before making a decision about continuing to see her. She knew he expected a woman who'd never lain with a man, inexperienced, and chaste.

Her one time with Edmund had been quick and unsatisfying, leaving Francesca with doubts about making love a second time. Nothing about their coupling had made her feel desired or loved. As it turned out, she never had to worry about going through the experience with him again.

"This isn't easy for me to talk about, Zeke." Keeping her back straight, chin jutted out, she refused to allow herself to be seen as a victim. She'd agreed to Edmund's request. The fact she regretted the brash action no longer mattered. Losing the baby had been a harsh punishment.

"Take your time. There's no need to rush."

Pursing her lips, she shifted her gaze outside. As the minutes ticked by, a sick feeling began to grow deep in her stomach. Inhaling a slow breath, she forced herself to look at Zeke. He'd leaned toward her, features earnest as he waited for her to explain.

Ignoring the lump in her throat, she squared her shoulders, forcing herself to meet his gaze. "I've told you a little about Edmund."

Disgust twisted Zeke's mouth. "A man I hope to never meet."

"There was a little more to what happened than him ending our betrothal. The real reason I left New York." Standing, she walked to the other side of the room, heart pounding. Turning to face him, she spoke before her courage disappeared.

"I made a horrible mistake. It happened not long after accepting his proposal." Tearing her gaze from his, she stared at the floor. "I..." Francesca couldn't look at him. Refused to see the condemnation when he learned the truth. "I ended up with child, Zeke."

When he stared, not responding, she took a couple tentative steps toward him. "Zeke?"

Clearing his throat, he didn't move from his spot on the sofa. "Where is the child?"

Face paling, tears formed in her eyes. "I was almost four months along when I lost it." The last words were choked out on a sob.

Standing, he closed the distance between them, taking her in his arms. "I'm sorry you had to go through that, sweetheart. So sorry." Holding her, he stroked her back, letting her cry it out.

Several minutes passed before she lifted her head, swiping at the wetness on her face. "I soaked your shirt."

Sliding strands of hair behind her ear, his grin was filled with warmth. "It'll dry."

"I don't know what came over me, Zeke. Crying over losing the baby stopped a long time ago." Although the lingering depression didn't. Francesca knew the tears were partly due to fear over his reaction to her news.

Taking her hand, he walked to the sofa, sitting her down beside him. When she didn't meet his gaze, Zeke gently gripped her chin, lifting her face toward his.

"If you think what happened is going to change my mind about us, you're wrong, Frannie." Skimming a kiss across her lips, he dropped his hand. The confusion on her face would've made him chuckle if the reason for her grief wasn't so heartrending. "Edmund was a fool for letting you go. What happened between the two of you is in the past. What I hope you and I have is a future." Running his knuckles down her cheek, he followed the action with a kiss.

Kansas City, Missouri

Melvin Merck rested clasped hands on his ample stomach, leaning back in his office chair. At three on a late fall afternoon, the air was still stifling. He'd long ago loosened the string tie around his neck, released the top button of his shirt, and kicked off the leather shoes he'd ordered from New York. This was the best he could do until arriving home to soak in a cold bath.

Melvin's weary gaze landed on the papers he'd been reading. *Last Will and Testament of Kyle Forshew*. If all went as planned, the simple change Kyle had agreed to would make an immeasurable difference in the lawyer's solitary life.

Melvin had added a simple clause allowing the lawyer authority to name an organization who'd receive proceeds from the estate if none of the beneficiaries were living. At the time, neither expected the clause to be executed. Then Kyle was murdered, and Melvin's mind began working through a variety of scenarios. Each option benefited him.

Illegal? Probably. Unethical? Absolutely.

The telegram from Francesca O'Reilly had confirmed what Melvin suspected. Both Louis Elder and Nellie Crawford were in Splendor, although their accommodations couldn't be more different. Elder had been arrested for setting off an explosion in the building where Nellie lived. She was recuperating from injuries sustained in the blast.

The ability to take control of Kyle's estate was now within his power. A quick telegram to the man holed up in Big Pine initiated the plan. By now, the gunslinger would be in Splendor, awaiting Melvin's next order.

Once the two were dead, Melvin would wait an appropriate period before naming an organization to receive the estate proceeds. A corporation outside of Kansas City that he controlled.

"Are you certain this is a good idea, Dax?" Rachel Pelletier carried a blanket to the wagon she, Shining Star, and Bull's wife, Lydia, would take to town. Billy, Bull, and Dax would accompany them on horseback.

The trip had two purposes. The ranch needed supplies, and it was time Doc McCord examined Shining Star. With Rachel by his side, Billy had done his best to explain to Shining Star what would happen at the clinic.

During her short time at the ranch, Shining Star had come to rely on Billy, their friendship growing. It was rare to see her without him being close by.

The ranch hands knew to keep watch for the band of renegade Crow. Either they didn't know Running Bear had escorted his granddaughter to the ranch, or they were being cautious, planning a raid to abduct Shining Star. Dax, Billy, and Bull believed the latter.

"The Crow aren't going to attack us in daylight, Rachel. We need supplies, and you're the one to mention Shining Star should have an examination. We'll be back at the ranch well before sunset." Dax glanced at the small group. "Climb on up, sweetheart. We'll head out when you're settled."

Taking his hand, Rachel sat between Lydia and Shining Star, picking up the lines. "Are you two ready?"

Lydia nodded, Shining Star stared straight ahead, eyes wide, hands clasped in her lap. Slapping the lines,

Rachel guided the wagon out of the ranch entrance, entering the trail to town.

Lydia and Rachel kept up a continual stream of conversation during the ride, Shining Star listening without responding. The older women believed she understood a good deal more English than she let on.

Good weather and a trail not yet rutted out from the winter storms, they crossed the town boundary sooner than expected. Deciding to stop at the clinic first, Dax led the group to Worthington Street.

The town leaders had finally named the various roads inside the town, naming the one with the clinic after Doctor Charles Worthington. Rachel's uncle, he'd been the first doctor in Splendor. With plans to retire soon, Charles, Clay McCord, and the town had begun a search for his replacement.

Helping the women down, they entered the clinic, glad for the empty front room. "Doc McCord?" Dax knocked on the exam room doors, then called again from the base of the stairs.

"Clay's out for a spell." Doctor Worthington came down the stairs, his steps slowing when he spotted an Indian woman. "Who do we have here?"

"This is Shining Star. She's Running Bear's granddaughter," Dax said.

Approaching her, the doctor smiled. "Does she speak English?"

"A little," Billy answered. "Rachel explained what to expect, but we don't know how much she understood."

"I understand." Shining Star surprised them all by speaking up.

Chuckling, Doc Worthington motioned for her to follow. "Rachel, would you be available to assist me?"

She'd left New York years before to work with her uncle in his clinic. After marrying Dax and having children, she'd trained someone to take her place before trimming her hours. She now helped out when there was an emergency.

"Of course, Doctor. Dax, do you want to stay or start loading supplies?"

Billy crossed his arms, planting his feet. "I want to stay."

Sending an amused look at Bull, Dax nodded. "Seems we'll be staying, Rachel."

"This won't take long, Dax. There's coffee upstairs. Help yourselves." Worthington opened the door to the exam room. "Shall we get started?"

Bill Short rested his arms on the bar at the Dixie, nursing a whiskey. He'd been in Splendor for two days, spending the hours locating the two people of interest to him.

Short had never been this far west in the Montana Territory. His work generally kept him in the Dakotas, Colorado, Kansas, Nebraska, or Missouri. To his surprise, he liked the isolation Splendor provided.

"Another?" Paul, the longtime Dixie bartender, wiped down the bar. He'd been watching the newcomer since he'd come in a couple days before. Short asked few questions, and never made a move to join a table for cards or company.

He held out his glass. "One more."

Paul studied him as he lifted the bottle and poured. "You plan on settling in Splendor?"

"Haven't decided. I understand the town's been growing." Taking a sip, he set the glass down.

"That it has. We've got some big ranches if that interests you." Paul's gaze locked on the pearl handled six-shooter around the man's waist. He'd spotted it the first time Short had entered the Dixie, pegging him as more of a gunslinger than ranch hand.

"Might be interested."

"Let me know and I'll give you a couple names." Paul ambled away, not for the first time wondering if Bill Short was the man's real name.

Approaching a table where three men played cards, Paul lowered his voice, bending enough so Cash Coulter could hear him. "There's a man at the bar named Bill Short. Something's not right about him." Straightening, he looked at the others. "Anything I can get you, gents?"

Nodding when they ordered more drinks, Paul returned to the bar. Several minutes passed before the deputy reacted to his words.

Finishing his hand, Cash scooped up his winnings and stood. "Well, gentlemen, I'd best get back to work. It's been a pleasure."

Going straight to the jail, Cash stalked inside, taking a seat opposite Gabe. "What do you know about Bill Short?"

"Can't say as I recognize the name. What's the reason?"

"Paul at the Dixie told me something's not quite right about him."

Rubbing his jaw, Gabe nodded. As far as he knew, Paul had expressed the same concern one other time. His unease had led Gabe and his deputies to arrest a man wanted for a series of bank robberies.

Opening a drawer, he pulled out a stack of wanted posters. Splitting them into two groups, he slid one pile toward Cash.

"Start looking."

Ten minutes later, Gabe handed Cash a poster. "He look familiar?"

A smile cracked the corners of Cash's mouth. "That's the man at the Dixie."

Standing, Gabe grabbed his hat before checking his six-shooter. "It's time we have a chat with William James Short."

Chapter Twenty-Five

"You said this would be a celebration supper, Aaron. What is it we're celebrating?" Francesca tipped the glass of wine to her lips, taking a sip.

Aaron invited Zeke and her to join him and Nancy at the Eagle's Nest for a special supper. After making small talk for almost half an hour, Zeke still hadn't joined them. The disappointment cut through her, the same as it had when he'd stopped calling on her.

Francesca hadn't seen him for more than a few minutes since explaining about the pregnancy. They'd both been busy, but Zeke had seemed distant and preoccupied. Maybe after considering what she'd said, he'd changed his mind, no longer having an interest in a woman who'd been with another man.

The thought angered her. Why was it all right for a man to sleep with different women before marriage, but not a woman? Edmund had been with several, and she had no doubt Zeke had also experienced his share of women.

"I hoped to wait until Zeke joined us, but it seems he's been delayed." Aaron had delivered the invitation for supper to Zeke at the jail, who'd accepted. "Given the time, perhaps we should proceed." His gaze moved to Nancy, the warmth passing between them triggering an ache in Francesca's chest. When Aaron opened his mouth to continue, a deep voice stopped him.

"Apologies for being late." Zeke placed a hand on Francesca's shoulder and squeezed before taking the seat next to her. "Have you already ordered?"

"Not yet." Aaron reached toward Nancy, taking her hand in his. "We were waiting for you."

"They have an announcement to make, Zeke." Francesca glanced at him, returning her attention to Nancy. By the look on her friend's face, she had a good idea what the couple wanted to share.

Holding up their joined hands, Aaron couldn't contain a smile. "Nancy has done me the great honor of agreeing to be my wife."

"How wonderful!" Francesca stood, hugging both of her friends, her joy at their decision sincere.

Zeke shook Aaron's hand before giving Nancy a brief embrace. "Great news. Will you marry in Splendor?"

Nancy glanced at Aaron before answering. "We're still deciding. It would be the perfect opportunity for my mother and brother to visit."

"Still, it's a long trip, and we have many friends in New York." Aaron's lips thinned before he picked up his glass of wine. "We both love Splendor, but most of my business interests are back east."

"You could get married twice," Francesca said. "Once in front of your friends here, and the other for those in New York."

"It's not a *bad* idea, Aaron. I'm certain Frannie and the other friends I've made would help with the arrangements."

"We'd love to help, Nancy. Nothing has to be complicated. How soon would you want the ceremony?"

"Tomorrow." Aaron chuckled, kissing the back of Nancy's hand. "It's October. We need to leave for New York before mid-November to miss the worst of the winter weather."

"That will give us more than enough time to plan the ceremony and reception." Francesca reached for her reticule, stopping at the feel of Zeke's hand on her arm.

"Why don't you and Nancy work on the details tomorrow. Tonight, we'll celebrate her and Aaron's engagement." Lifting his wine glass, Zeke's eyes gleamed. "To Nancy and Aaron. May their future together be long and filled with love."

Zeke threaded his fingers through Francesca's, taking the long way to her house, surprised to discover they were alone. Aaron had insisted Nancy move out of Francesca's house and take a room at the St. James. Zeke suspected the decision had to do with giving both couples more privacy.

"I'm sorry about being late to supper. Gabe called all the deputies to the jail for a meeting."

Francesca lifted her gaze to meet his. "It must have been important."

"The bartender at the Dixie alerted Cash to a man who seemed suspicious. Cash and Gabe checked wanted posters."

She lifted a brow. "There was one for him?"

"Yes. By the time they got to the Dixie, the man was gone. Gabe wants us to keep watch for him."

"What's his name?"

For a moment, he forgot her profession encouraged questions. "William James Short. He goes by Bill Short. He's wanted for robbery and murder."

They walked several more feet before Francesca spoke again. "I wonder why he's in Splendor. I'd expect a hired gun and robber to stay closer to larger cities in more populated states. We have one bank and are served by daily stage service. Which means…" Her voice trailed off as the realization why he might be in Splendor became clear.

"Harmon Tibbs was murdered with a Bowie knife and we still haven't found the killer. Louis Elder is in jail for his attempt to kill Beauty. Now, Bill Short." Zeke stopped at the end of the boardwalk, staring at a sky spotted with millions of stars and waning moon. "We don't know who he's after, but I'm convinced the trip to Splendor wasn't a random decision."

Francesca's grip on Zeke's hand tightened. "What if Louis Elder hired him?"

"Possible, but why would Elder go after Beauty if he'd already hired a skilled killer?" A sound from outside the boardinghouse caught his attention. "Stay here, Frannie."

Drawing his gun, Zeke walked along the side of the building to the back, stopping when he heard the noise again. Glancing behind him, he sent Francesca a hard glare when she moved to join him. Shaking his head, he continued along the back wall of the boardinghouse.

A small smile tilted the corners of his mouth at the sight of a ladder leaning against the building. His gaze moved up the rungs, halting on booted feet near the top. Raising his gun, he pointed it at the man attempting to open a window.

"Stop what you're doing and drop your gun."

Instead of heeding Zeke's weapon, the man shifted on the ladder. Pointing the gun toward the ground, he fired, missing the deputy by inches. Firing again, he tried again to open the window and crawl inside.

Raising his arm, Zeke aimed and fired. A pitiful groan preceded a gun dropping to the ground. Seconds later, a body, arms flailing, thudded feet away from Zeke. Holding his weapon on the body, he walked forward.

Getting no reaction when he kicked the legs with a boot, Zeke knelt down, checking the pulse. Hearing shoes crunching on the dry earth, he raised his gun, lowering it when Francesca peaked around the corner.

"Are you all right?"

"I'm fine, Frannie. This one isn't doing so good."

Moving closer, she couldn't miss the odd angle of the man's head. "Is he dead?"

"Yes. Broke his neck from the fall."

Shifting to get a better look at the man, her brows scrunched together. "Who is he, Zeke?"

"There's not enough light to tell. I'll need help to carry him back to the jail."

"I'll go." Francesca hurried off, heading toward the jail, halting at the ear-piercing scream from the front of the boardinghouse. Zeke took off, racing past her. Ignoring his warning to stay behind, she followed, stopping when he held up his hand.

"Stay right there." Staring up, his gaze landed on an open window.

"That's Beauty's room," Francesca shouted, rushing toward him. Disregarding his scowl, she tried the front door. "It's locked."

A second scream had Zeke kicking in the door at the same time someone turned up the oil lamps inside. Meeting the onsite manager at the base of the stairs, he raced up them, gripping his six-shooter.

Stopping at the top, he listened. The sound of something hard hitting one of the doors moved him to action. Kicking the door once, it slammed open. Inside, Beauty, blood streaming down her face, lay on the floor. A man stood over her.

"Stay where you are or I'll shoot her."

Lifting his gun, Zeke aimed at the man's chest. "You'll be dead before she is."

"You'd risk her life?" The man sneered at the same time a flash of fear twisted his features.

Zeke smirked. "I won't be."

Something in Zeke's voice must've warned the man. Not lowering his six-shooter, he took a slight step toward the open door. Thrusting his booted foot forward, the door slammed in Zeke's face.

Kicking it open, he spotted the man jumping out the window. Instead of following, he dropped down next to Beauty. The blood on her face was beginning to dry. A bruise formed around a swollen right eye, and both arms were wrapped around her waist in a protective gesture.

"Beauty. Can you hear me?"

Answering with a low moan, she rolled to her side, pulling her legs up.

Noticing movement behind him, Zeke saw the manager standing in the doorway. "Get the doctor."

"But I'm supposed to stay here."

Glaring, Zeke pointed at Beauty. "She's been beaten. Now you get the doctor or you may be looking for another job."

"Yeesss, sir."

Grabbing a blanket, he placed it over her, stroking her hair. "The doctor will be here soon, Beauty."

Her voice was low, thready. "Thank you."

Standing, he walked to the window, leaning outside. Expecting to see Beauty's attacker on the ground, he was stunned to see no one. Not a deputy and not Francesca. Confused, he scanned the street.

Bag in hand, Doc McCord ran across the street toward the boardinghouse. Returning to his spot next to

Beauty, Zeke rested a hand on her forehead, checking for a fever. The increased warmth worried him.

"What happened?" Clay knelt next to them, his hands running over her body.

"Pistol whipped and beaten. She's been holding her stomach, Doc."

"Beauty? Are you able to talk?"

Instead of speaking, she gave Clay a single nod.

"Good. Tell me why you're holding your stomach." He dabbed at the blood, tending to the cuts underneath.

Licking her lips, she opened her mouth. "Kicked me."

The words came out at the same time Gabe, Hawke, and Shane Banderas entered the room. Spotting Beauty, Hawke cursed, dropping to his knees.

"Did you get him?" Zeke searched their faces, seeing blank stares. "The man who did this to Beauty and jumped out the window?"

Gabe walked to the window, looking outside. "We didn't see anyone, Zeke."

"What about Francesca? She was waiting for me outside the boardinghouse."

Gabe whirled toward him. "Are you certain?"

"She was with me when we heard Beauty scream. I told her to stay downstairs while I came up here. Are you saying you didn't see her, either?"

Gabe glanced at the others, jaw clenched, before he rushed toward the stairs. "Francesca was gone."

Chapter Twenty-Six

"Francesca's disappeared." Zeke ran a shaky hand through his hair, still not able to accept she was gone.

Gabe had every available deputy search the town, even woke up Nick Barnett, Noah Brandt, and a couple of Redemption's Edge ranch hands who lived in town. Hours passed as they searched every building and spoke to dozens of people.

Hawke had carried Beauty to the clinic, refusing to leave her side until Gabe ordered him to join the search. Specifically, to use his tracking skills to look for Francesca. Travis Dixon, a Pelletier ranch hand who lived in town with his wife, Isabella, and also an expert tracker, would join Hawke.

"We *will* find her, Zeke, and whoever took her." Gabe spread out a map Noah and he had created showing the region around Splendor. Besides the town, ranches, and farms, it identified major landmarks, caves, lakes, creeks, and at Noah's insistence, the best fishing holes.

Gabe motioned for the deputies and volunteers to gather around his desk. "We'll form several small groups. Most will search the town again, including attics, basements, and private living spaces. The others will create a perimeter outside of town."

"She's still here, Gabe." Zeke stared at the map. "Bill Short took her and is holed up somewhere in Splendor.

We'd do better by having Hawke and Shane use their skills in town."

"What makes you think it's Short who took her?" Gabe asked.

"I wasn't sure until you passed around the wanted poster tonight. It was him inside Beauty's room."

"You're certain he's the one who beat her?" Hawke asked.

Zeke nodded. "No doubt. We were no more than ten feet apart. I got a real good look at him. What I don't understand is how he was able to jump from the window and grab Francesca without anyone seeing or hearing them. I can't believe she'd let herself be taken without a fight."

Hex stood next to him, nodding in agreement. "He must've had help."

Cash crossed his arms, leaning against the edge of the desk. "I'll talk to Paul at the Dixie, find out if Short has been talking to anyone."

"He's been staying in one of the rooms upstairs at Finn's," Mack added. "I'll speak with Finn and interview his ladies to see if they've seen Short with someone specific."

"Do you all agree with Zeke's belief Short has Francesca and they're still in Splendor?" Gabe asked. A series of nods and yeses provided the answer. "All right. For now, we'll concentrate on searching for them in town. Cash and Mack will talk to those in the saloons. Everyone ask around about Short having a partner or meeting up with anyone in particular. I know all of you have been up all night, but I'm asking you to work a few more hours. I'll write down a schedule so you all get a few hours of rest until we find Francesca."

Gabe spent a few more minutes dividing the men into groups before sending them off. "Zeke and Hex, I'd like you to stay."

"But—" Zeke's protest died on his lips when Gabe held up a hand.

"Our first priority is to find Francesca. The second is to arrest Short. I want him alive, gentlemen. Do you understand me?"

"You know we can't promise that, Gabe," Zeke answered for both of them. "If he shoots at us, we're going to fire back."

"Protect yourselves, but don't do anything stupid. We need to learn who hired Short and why he's in Splendor."

Francesca struggled to open her eyes, moaning at the throbbing pain in her jaw. Reaching out a hand to leverage herself up, she felt the hard wood floor. Pressing fingers to her temples, she tried to recall what happened, why she was on the floor in a room she didn't recognize.

Ignoring the pain, she shoved herself to a sitting position, resting her back against a nearby wall. Looking around, Francesca's stomach roiled as she recalled the night before.

She'd been with Zeke. It was dark, after supper with Nancy and Aaron. He'd rushed behind the boardinghouse at a strange sound. She recalled gunshots, a body on the ground, then a woman's scream. Zeke ran into the boardinghouse while Francesca remained outside. There was another scream, men shouting.

"Beauty's room," she murmured to herself, the pain growing worse.

She'd been ready to follow Zeke inside when a man jumped from the window, landing inches from her. That's when the memory ended, but not the odd pain in her jaw.

Touching it, she felt the swollen flesh. Another memory flashed in her mind. A meaty fist coming at her before everything turned black. Someone had hit her. A man. The same man who'd jumped from the second floor.

Her blood chilled, and not from the icy feel of the small room. The person who'd hit her had been the same man who'd threatened Beauty.

Blinking, she looked for a door, window, any way to escape. The room was no more than eight feet square with no windows. At first, she didn't spot a door, knowing one had to exist. Blinking again, she scanned the room once more, methodically moving a foot at a time when a door flew open. A man stood in the doorway, the light from the lantern blinding her.

"I see you're awake."

She scooted into the corner when he took a step toward her. "Who are you, and why am I here?" Francesca already had a good idea of who'd taken her.

"My name's not important. You're here to get what I really want."

Lifting her chin, she ignored the pain in her jaw. "Which is?"

"I'm here for Beauty and Louis Elder."

Adjusting her position, she hid a smirk. "Seems to me you ruined your chance for Beauty, and Elder is already behind bars. You might as well let me go and ride out, Mr..."

Not answering, he set down the lantern. Reaching behind him, he grabbed a plate with one hand, drawing his six-shooter with the other.

"Stay where you are while I set this down. If you try to escape, I'll tie you up."

Francesca considered trying to get past him, discarding the idea when he raised the gun.

"I don't have trouble killing a woman. You best think about that before doing something stupid." Setting the plate a few feet from her, he backed away. "You said Elder is in jail?"

"He tried to kill Beauty. Seems you're intent on doing the same. Why?" Scooting forward, she snagged a slice of bread, taking a small bite.

"The gal means a great deal of money to a friend of mine."

Francesca arched a brow, his meaning becoming clear. "Only if she's dead?"

"Now aren't you the smart one."

"Is it the same with Elder?"

"You sure ask a lot of questions, I don't like women who talk so much."

Did he think she cared what kind of women he liked? "I don't like men who kidnap me, Mr. Short."

His brows rose at the use of his name. "How do you know who I am?"

"I heard about you from one of the deputies, who learned it from the sheriff. Do you know what that means? Your identity is not a secret. They'll be coming straight for you. Trust me, you won't be spending time in the territorial prison. You'll hang."

Throwing back his head, he laughed. "Do you know how many times I've been told I'm going to hang? More than you can count." He touched his neck. "They haven't caught me yet."

"If you want to keep your record clean, I'd suggest you forget about Beauty and Louis, and get out of here."

A bell ringing caught both of their attention. Excitement tore through Francesca. It was the church bell, the one the town installed after the original building burned down. She wasn't in some remote location. Short had taken refuge in town.

"We're done talking. Eat your food, and don't do anything to get yourself shot." Backing out the door, Short slammed it shut, locking it.

"Wait!" She held her breath for tense seconds, but he didn't return. Francesca had been so close to talking him into leaving.

Munching on the piece of bread, she picked up the cup of coffee. She grimaced at the tepid brew, deciding it was better than nothing. Finishing both the bread and coffee, she shoved herself up, determined to find a way out of this prison.

"Has anyone checked Noah's warehouse?" Zeke's fisted hands rested on his hips as he turned in a circle.

Hex looked up the street to the building Noah used to house extra materials and furnishings for his houses. "It was one of the first places he checked after Francesca was taken."

"I want to go through it once more. Let's find Noah and get the key." Zeke didn't wait for Hex to respond before rushing down the street to the last place they'd seen him.

Noah didn't hesitate to go with the brothers to his warehouse. Packed with leftover building material and furniture he'd purchased from families no longer needing the items.

Pulling the door open, Noah entered first. There were few windows, making it difficult for anyone unfamiliar with the building to find their way around.

"If she's in here, it would be in one of the back rooms." Noah slid between the stacks of furniture.

Reaching the back, he opened the first door. Zeke pushed past him. The room was as packed as the front. They moved to the next door, finding nothing. The same with the third.

Turning toward Zeke and Hex, Noah shook his head. "She isn't here."

"Any other place we may have missed?" Rubbing the back of his neck, Zeke began to feel the first pricks of frustration.

So far, he'd been able to stay positive, his instincts convincing him Short and Francesca were still in town. She wasn't who the gunslinger wanted. The hired gun had come to town for Beauty, who was now hidden in an upstairs examination room at the clinic.

Her boss, Ruby, sat outside the room with a shotgun resting across her lap. One of her bartenders had been posted downstairs with instructions to only allow Gabe or his deputies inside.

"Wait." Noah hurried back through the front room, motioning for them to follow. Locking the front door, he continued past the warehouse to a rundown shack. "I know it doesn't look like much now, but at one time, it was a busy saloon. On both sides were tents for the ladies to entertain the miners and ranch hands."

"My wife and I own it now. We haven't been inside for years, but as I recall, there are some rooms in the back. Real small. As long as it's been, there's probably nothing more than critters inhabiting them."

"The perfect place to hide someone." Zeke's heart pounded faster as Noah moved to the door.

He glanced around, pointing to the lock and chain on the ground. Lowering his voice, Noah slipped his gun from its holster, waiting as the others did the same.

Without a word, he nodded for them to move behind him. Holding the six-shooter straight out, Noah lifted his boot. With one swift kick, the rotted door burst off its hinges. Noah twisted, jumping back at the same time bullets flew through the opening.

Chapter Twenty-Seven

"Get back." Noah didn't have to do more before Zeke and Hex dropped down, moving away from the open doorway. "Don't know if it's Short, but it *is* someone who doesn't want us here."

"It's Short," Zeke answered, rising to look through a dirt-encrusted window, falling back when a bullet ripped through the glass. The three were on the same side of the opening, making communication easier.

"See anything?" Hex asked.

"Nothing, but it's him. Which means Frannie is with him." Zeke shifted to look at Noah. "Is there another way inside?"

"Around back."

Zeke looked at his brother. "Hex, come with me. Noah, you stay here and guard the front."

With a nod, Noah checked the bullets in his six-shooter, settling back on his haunches. "He won't get past me."

They knew he meant it. A crack sharpshooter in the Union Army, Noah was a man you didn't underestimate. He was also someone you wanted on your side.

Zeke's heart hammered in his chest as he and Hex circled around to the back. It took a minute to find the door covered by the thick growth around it. Dirt and rock were piled around the base of the door.

"It's going to take time to get it open," Hex gritted out, showing the same sense of urgency as Zeke.

"Look for a window." Zeke hurried along the back wall before returning to Hex. "Nothing. We'll have to use the door."

A burst of gunfire from the front hurried their movements. Using their boots, they kicked aside the dirt and rock from the base of the door. Another volley of bullets helped cover the sound from their efforts. They tugged at the old handle, ripping it open.

Guns aimed in front of them, Zeke entered first, Hex right behind. The room was dark, cobwebs thick. The ground had never been covered with wood flooring, encouraging varmints to nest.

"Look." Zeke motioned at an inside door. Moving to it, he released the latch. Both held their breath as he cracked it open a couple inches.

Peeking into the adjoining room, a feral grin appeared on Zeke's face, recognizing the gunslinger. He glanced over his shoulder. "It's Short."

Another round of bullets hit the wall near Zeke, moving him to action. Rather than draw back from the bullets, he slammed the door open, aimed at Short, and fired.

One hit the man's shoulder, shoving him backward against the wall. Walking forward, Zeke pointed the six-shooter at his chest.

"Where's Francesca?"

Instead of answering, Short sneered. "Who?"

Another bullet left Zeke's revolver, hitting the man's gun hand. His six-shooter fell to the ground, along with a string of curses.

Features hardening, Zeke raised the gun even with Short's face. "Where is Francesca?"

Raising his head, the outlaw's bloodshot eyes meet the deputy's, his mouth twisted into a hate-filled smirk. "Up and died on me."

Jaw tight, Zeke moved closer, touching his gun to Short's forehead. "One more chance to tell me the truth. I don't have a problem ending your life, Short." He glanced at the front door, seeing Noah, who offered a grim nod. "Where is she?"

"Might as well kill me, Deputy, because I'm not telling you anything."

Patience exhausted, Zeke's gun hand shook, the barrel digging into Short's forehead. Finger on the trigger, he began to pull at the same time a pair of strong hands gripped his shoulders.

"Back away, brother." Hex tugged him backward, taking the gun from his hand. "He will hang for all he's done, and we're going to find Frannie."

A cackle burst from Short, his shoulders shaking with laughter. Before Zeke could break from Hex's hold and slam a fist into the man's face, Noah pinned Short's arms behind him, binding them with a leather strap. When finished, Noah forced him to sit on the ground.

"I'll take him to Gabe. You boys keep looking. I'll return with more men." Clutching Short's collar, Noah dragged him up, shoving the killer out the door.

Zeke blew out a curse, slamming a hand on the wall. "Nothing. She's not here."

"Don't give up." Hex ran his hand over the wall again, searching for a secret door or latch, anything to indicate a hidden room. "Look at this room, then the other two. We're missing about eight feet of space."

Zeke let out a sigh, nodding. "You're right. What bothers me is we've been pounding on the walls, making plenty of noise, and not once have we heard her yell out."

"He may have gagged her." Hex turned when Caleb, Mack, and Beth Evans entered the shack.

"Gabe sent us to help search," Caleb explained. "Find anything yet?"

"Nothing," Zeke blew out.

Hex rested his hand on a wall. "We believe she's in a hidden room behind this wall."

"No matter what we do, we can't find a door," Zeke added.

"That's easy. I'll be right back." Mack left, returning a few minutes later carrying two sledgehammers. "Noah doesn't care if we tear the place down." Handing one to Caleb, they moved past Zeke and Hex to the wall.

It didn't take long to break the boards, exposing a poorly built rock wall. "I'll be. How do we get through that?" Hex asked.

Holding out his hand, Zeke took the sledgehammer from Mack. Entering the room next to the one they were attempting to enter, he swung. A moment later, Hex joined him with the other tool. As the others watched, they took little time to break down the wall.

Their spirits sank. At first, all they saw was another rock wall. Frustrated, Zeke continued to swing at the remaining wood wall. As the boards splintered away, hidden hinges emerged.

"How did we miss this?" Zeke asked, not expecting an answer as he continued breaking down the wall.

Directly behind the hidden door was a second one built into the rock wall. Dropping the sledgehammer, Zeke tried to open the door, pounding on it when it didn't open.

"Francesca! Francesca, can you hear me?"

"Move out of the way, Zeke." Hex swung twice, tearing the door from its hinges. Inside, a small form huddled in a corner.

Pushing past him, Zeke rushed into the room, dropping down to wrap his arms around her. "Francesca?" Pressing kisses to her forehead, his gaze moved over her. "Francesca, can you hear me?"

Turning toward him, relief passed over her face. "I knew you'd find me, Zeke."

Tightening his hold around her, he kissed her temple. "I never would've stopped looking. Are you ready to get out of here?" Her tired smile tore at his heart.

"More than ready."

Two days passed while Francesca and Beauty rested, healing from their ordeal with Bill Short. It had taken a great deal of questioning before the gunman confessed the name of the man who'd hired him.

Melvin Merck had been stunned when the sheriff and two deputies entered his office in Kansas City. The arrest had made headlines in a hundred mile radius. When the charges of hiring a gunslinger to murder two people in Montana became public, not a single person had come to his aid.

The trial had been swift, the trip to the Missouri State Penitentiary finalizing his humiliation. Two similar trials had been held in Big Pine. One for Louis Elder and his attempt to kill Beauty, as well as others at the Palace explosion. The second for Bill Short. U.S. Marshal Chan Evans had accompanied both men to the prison near Deer Lodge. None of the three would leave their confinement during their lifetimes.

Gabe and Zeke made the trip to the Tibbs ranch after arresting Short. They had little hope of finding the gunslinger, but talking to the ranch hand might provide valuable information. What they found sickened them.

From the signs, a Crow raiding party had attacked the ranch. The one hand had been killed where he sat on the front porch from a single arrow to his heart.

Circling buzzards drew their attention to a spot a hundred yards away. Wes Acker, his shirt and boots missing, had been staked out, the varmints finishing what the Crow raiders had started. He'd been dead several days before Gabe and Zeke found the remains.

Not far away, Gabe discovered saddlebags hidden in thick brush. Going through them, he removed an almost unused Bowie knife, along with over three thousand dollars.

"Seems we have answers to who killed Tibbs and attacked you." Repacking the saddlebags, Gabe secured them to his horse before mounting for the ride back to town. He'd send men out to retrieve the bodies and arrange proper burials.

The dangers behind them for now, Zeke knew the time had come to move forward with his plans.

Chapter Twenty-Eight

Francesca took the pen from Beauty's shaking hand, finalizing the documents needed to accept the proceeds of Kyle Forshew's estate. Given all that had transpired, it had taken longer than normal to close the estate. According to Horace Clausen, Beauty would soon be a wealthy woman. At her insistence, it would be a long time before the people of Splendor would learn of her change in station.

Standing, Francesca walked around the desk. "What are you going to do now?"

In her usual quiet nature, Beauty's serene features gave away nothing. "Nothing will change for a while. I'll be living in one of Noah's houses with two other girls. As soon as the Palace is finished, I'll serve drinks, the same as before."

"You don't plan to move back to the Palace?"

"Not now. Maybe never." Mouth drawing into a straight line, Beauty thought about her answer. "I hope to find work somewhere else."

"You do realize you no longer have to work."

"Yes, but I need to do something. I doubt the church women would welcome me into their circle."

Placing a hand on Beauty's arm, Francesca squeezed. "You would be surprised. Reverend Paige's wife, Ruth, welcomes everyone, no matter what has happened in the past. When you're ready, I'll host you and Ruth for lunch."

"You'd do that?"

"Of course. I hope you see me as your friend, Beauty. If there's anything I can do for you, please let me know."

A few minutes later, Francesca closed the door behind her. The last client of the day. Nancy had left early with Aaron.

Returning to her desk, she collected Beauty's signed documents, locking them in her safe. Sitting back down, she thought of the upcoming weekend. She'd become accustomed to having supper and spending time with Zeke on Fridays. They'd had lunch the day before, but she hadn't heard from or seen him since. She tried not to think about the depth of her disappointment.

Gathering her belongings, she walked downstairs, taking the back door out of the building. Using the shortest route to her house, Francesca tried to remember if she had anything to eat at home. Biscuits, part of a dried apple pie, sweet bread Nancy made. Not the best combination, but it would have to do.

Opening the front door, her jaw dropped and she came to an abrupt stop. Wildflowers were everywhere. The smells of supper drifted toward her from the kitchen. Zeke stood at the stove wearing what appeared to be a new shirt, clean pants, and boots with a distinct shine. Dropping her reticule and hat on a chair, she took a few tentative steps forward.

"What are you doing?"

One side of his mouth tilted upward into a half-smile. "Making supper."

She continued toward him, stopping a few feet away. "I see that. But why?"

Shrugging, he set the spoon down, turning to face her. "We need to eat, and I knew you'd be tired after working all day."

Glancing around, she motioned toward the vases. "And the flowers?"

"Do you like them? It took me a good part of the day to find enough to fill the room. I guess this isn't the best time of year for them."

Heart hammering, she fought the moisture forming in her eyes, finding it hard to take a full breath. "I love the flowers."

This time, he graced her with a broad smile. "Sit down and talk to me while supper finishes."

Francesca felt as if she'd walked into a world of fantasy, something from one of the children's books Christina read to Cici and Lucy. This couldn't be real, could it?

Sitting down, she drew one of the vases toward her, admiring the flowers. "These are lovely."

He didn't answer as he checked on the biscuits in the cast iron skillet. "Were you able to settle everything with Beauty?"

"Yes. It was odd, though." She explained how Beauty didn't want her new wealth to be known around town, and her decision to return to the Palace. "I expected a different reaction."

Transferring the biscuits to a bowl, he set it on the table. "Beauty isn't like any woman I've ever met. She goes her own way. It will be interesting to see how Hawke handles it."

Brows drawing together, she moved a hand toward the bowl, meaning to steal a biscuit before pulling it back. "Hawke?"

Eyes narrowing on her, he shook his head. "Never mind. Are you ready to eat?"

"Starving."

Chuckling, he set the pot on the already set table. Leaning down, he brushed a kiss across her mouth before sitting next to her.

"My mother used to make this at home in New Orleans. She didn't have a name for it. I tried to remember all the ingredients, but I may have gotten some wrong." Serving both of them, he waited until she tasted it.

"This is wonderful, Zeke. You'll have to show me how to make it."

They spoke of small matters, the need for more deputies, Francesca's search for another attorney, Aaron and Nancy's decision to marry in Splendor before returning to New York. When finished, they cleaned up before he took her hand.

"Would you walk with me?"

"I'd love to, Zeke."

For Francesca, their walk tonight felt different from those of the last few weeks. They were free of the threats hovering over the town. Beauty was safe, the men trying to kill her behind bars, the mystery of Harmon Tibbs's death solved. At least for a little while, the townsfolk could rest in peace.

Crossing the street toward the church, she slipped her arm through his. "Reverend Paige is going to marry Aaron and Nancy next weekend. Suzanne and some of the other women have volunteered to cook for the reception. It's hard to think of Nancy leaving. I've grown accustomed to her being in Splendor."

Looking down at her, he covered her hand with his. "Aaron plans to bring her back for a long visit once a year, Frannie. We can also travel east to see them."

It took a moment for his words to register. "We?"

"I've never been to New York. Accompanying you would be my chance to see it with someone who knows the city."

"Oh." Francesca felt an odd letdown at his explanation.

Continuing down the street, Zeke slowed in front of the Emporium window. "I've heard Josie and Olivia are doing well with the store."

"They are. Nancy bought her dress for the wedding from them. It was designed by Allie Coulter. She does beautiful work."

Moving along, Zeke tightened his hold on her arm, staring straight ahead. "I'll never have much money,

Frannie. I'm saving for a small ranch outside of town, but it will be years before there's enough to buy the land and the cattle."

A lump formed in her throat. What was he trying to tell her? Was he ending their courtship because of his financial situation?

"I'm not interested in a wealthy man, Zeke. If I commit to a man, it will be to someone I love."

He said nothing for several long moments, causing her chest to constrict. The silence told her as much as his words.

"You believe that now, Frannie. Will you feel the same when you're ready to marry and have children? You'll want more for them than what a deputy in a small frontier town could ever provide."

Crossing the large expanse of open space between the boardinghouse and school, he led them to the creek. Soon, the rain and winter snows would arrive, raising the water to almost overflowing.

Stopping at the creek's edge, the silence continued, both staring into the water. Her heart pounded in a painful rhythm. She'd thought they were moving in the same direction, toward a future together. His words tonight didn't bode well for a shared life.

Walking into her house earlier, seeing the flowers and eating his wonderful supper, her hopes had soared. She couldn't think of a man who'd go to so much trouble for a woman he didn't want in his life. Then again, she'd never been good at understanding the reasons behind Zeke's actions.

Guiding her away from the creek, they walked along the edge before turning toward the bench. He stopped within inches of it, as if deciding what to do next.

"Do you care to sit for a while, Frannie?"

Ignoring her jumbled thoughts, she nodded, taking a seat at one end. Instead of sitting next to her, he paced away, turning to face the water. Biting her bottom lip, she waited, not wanting to rush whatever it was he planned to say.

A sense of foreboding claimed her. Instead of shirking away, afraid of what he'd say, she squared her shoulders. Whatever came next, she'd accept it with grace and dignity.

Turning toward Francesca, his face gave nothing away. Eyes locked on hers, he took the few steps back to the bench where she sat, chin lifted, back straight. Before registering what was happening, Zeke dropped down on one knee.

"I love you, Frannie. Have since the day you stepped off the stagecoach. I'll never be good enough for you, never be able to provide all you deserve." Seeing the shock on her face, the tears welling in her eyes, he reached out, taking her hands in his. "With all my faults, I'm asking you to share my life, build a family and a future with me. Marry me, Frannie. I promise no one will ever love you as much as me."

Breath coming in soft gulps, she stared at him, stunned into silence. After a few tense moments, she realized he waited for an answer.

Pulling a hand from hers, Zeke swiped at the lone tear streaking down her cheek. "Frannie?"

Finding her voice, a radiant smile lit her face. "I love you, too. Yes, I'll marry you. Yes, yes, yes."

Epilogue

One week later...

Francesca held Zeke's hand, glancing at the unexpected crowd in the church's community room. It surprised her how many people came to celebrate Aaron and Nancy's wedding.

A few minutes earlier, they'd said their vows in front of Reverend Paige, tying their lives together before returning to New York to do it all again. Coming a few weeks after the trials of three killers, the celebration of their union came at the perfect time.

"It won't be long before you'll be saying your own vows." Rachel Pelletier stood beside her, Dax on the other side talking with Zeke. "Ruth Paige said her husband has agreed to a ceremony on Christmas Eve."

"We thought since most of our friends will be in town for services that night, they wouldn't mind him including our vows."

"It's an excellent idea, Frannie. The services are held at three in the afternoon, which gives those out of town time to return home before it gets too late. The women are already discussing what to cook for the celebration afterward. They're all excited for you two."

Leaning over, she hugged Rachel. "I'm so glad you talked me into coming to Splendor."

"So am I. Dax tells me you've been looking for another lawyer to join you. Any luck?"

Francesca's eyes lit with excitement. "There's a man in California who's shown an interest. In fact, he sent a telegram saying he'd be here before Thanksgiving to talk in person. His experience is perfect. He's riding out with a couple of ranchers who want to take a look at the area."

"Be sure to have them speak with Dax and Luke."

Smiling, Francesca's attention shifted to across the room. "I plan to. What do you think of Hawke and Beauty?"

Following her gaze, Rachel watched as the couple moved through the food line, talking as they filled their plates. "I haven't given it any thought. Hawke is an excellent deputy. Somewhat surly and hard-edged. I know little of Beauty, beyond her being the target of killers."

"She lives in one of Noah's houses with two other women, and serves drinks at the Palace. Or she will once it reopens next week. She's quiet, smart, and wants to make a life in Splendor." Francesca wouldn't mention the wealth the young woman had recently acquired.

"It would make an interesting match."

"Indeed, it would." Francesca shot a smile at Zeke, getting one in return. "How is Shining Star doing?"

"Fine. She's learning English much faster than I expected, and her pregnancy is going well." Rachel let out a sigh, shaking her head. "I feel awful for her. She doesn't want to stay at the ranch, but Running Bear has forbid her from returning to the village. It's sad and not right, but as the chief, it's his decision."

"It's fortunate she has a place to stay. There isn't a better place for her than your ranch. Is Billy still guarding her?"

"He is, and isn't at all happy about it," Rachel answered. "Unfortunately, Shining Star isn't comfortable with anyone else, and Dax is certain the Crow will be coming for her. Especially after what Gabe and Zeke found at the Tibbs ranch. Dax told me about the ranch hand and Wes Acker."

"Gabe is certain it was Crow raiders. It's miles away from your ranch, but it shows they aren't afraid of coming after anyone."

"And they want Shining Star." A booming voice at the front door drew Francesca's attention. Rachel chuckled, recognizing who entered. "It seems Baron Klaussner has returned from Europe with his son."

"Baron Klaussner?"

"That's right. You arrived after he left for his trip," Rachel answered. "He came to Splendor a few years ago. His close friend from New York, Walter Evans, Gabe and Chan's father, was already here. You'll like him. In fact, he'll be pleased to have a new attorney in town."

"Is he married?"

"No. I intend to introduce him to the women who traveled from New York with you. A supper at the ranch. Maybe Thanksgiving. You and Zeke will be invited."

"Are you ready to get something to eat, darlin'?" Zeke slipped an arm over Francesca's shoulders, pulling her close.

"I'm starving."

"As always," Zeke joked, dropping his arm to take her hand. "Aaron and Nancy have invited us to join them for supper tonight at the Eagle's Nest. They leave tomorrow on the stage. I told them we'd be there."

Leaning up, she kissed his chin. "Thank you."

Walking toward the food table, their attention caught on the couple sitting alone at a corner table. Hawke and Beauty. Both were quiet, her attention focused on the food in front of her, his on Beauty.

Francesca squeezed Zeke's hand, nodding toward them. "What do you think?"

He studied the couple a moment before his gaze landed on his fiancée. "I think the next few months are going to be real entertaining."

Thank you for taking the time to read Thunder Valley. If you enjoyed it, please consider telling your friends or posting a short review. Word of mouth is an author's best friend and much appreciated.

Watch for book seventeen in the Redemption Mountain series, ***A Very Splendor Christmas***.

If you want in on all the backstage action of my historical westerns, join my VIP Readers Group.

Join my Newsletter to be notified of Pre-Orders and New Releases:
https://www.shirleendavies.com/

I care about quality, so if you find an error, please contact me via email at
shirleen@shirleendavies.com

About the Author

Shirleen Davies writes romance. She is the best-selling author of books in the romantic suspense, military romance, historical western romance, and contemporary western romance genres. Shirleen grew up in Southern California, attended Oregon State University, and has degrees from San Diego State University and the University of Maryland. Her passion is writing emotionally charged stories of flawed people who find redemption through love and acceptance. She lives with her husband in a beautiful town in northern Arizona.

I love to hear from my readers!

Send me an email: shirleen@shirleendavies.com
Visit my Website: https://www.shirleendavies.com/
Sign up to be notified of New Releases:
https://www.shirleendavies.com/
Follow me on Amazon:
http://www.amazon.com/author/shirleendavies
Follow me on BookBub:
https://www.bookbub.com/authors/shirleen-davies

Other ways to connect with me:

Facebook Author Page:
http://www.facebook.com/shirleendaviesauthor
Twitter: www.twitter.com/shirleendavies

Pinterest: http://pinterest.com/shirleendavies
Instagram:
https://www.instagram.com/shirleendavies_author/

Books by Shirleen Davies

Historical Western Romance Series

Redemption Mountain

Redemption's Edge, Book One
Wildfire Creek, Book Two
Sunrise Ridge, Book Three
Dixie Moon, Book Four
Survivor Pass, Book Five
Promise Trail, Book Six
Deep River, Book Seven
Courage Canyon, Book Eight
Forsaken Falls, Book Nine
Solitude Gorge, Book Ten
Rogue Rapids, Book Eleven
Angel Peak, Book Twelve
Restless Wind, Book Thirteen
Storm Summit, Book Fourteen
Mystery Mesa, Book Fifteen
Thunder Valley, Book Sixteen
A Very Splendor Christmas, Book Seventeen, Coming Next
in the Series!

MacLarens of Boundary Mountain

Colin's Quest, Book One,
Brodie's Gamble, Book Two
Quinn's Honor, Book Three
Sam's Legacy, Book Four
Heather's Choice, Book Five

Nate's Destiny, Book Six
Blaine's Wager, Book Seven
Fletcher's Pride, Book Eight
Bay's Desire, Book Nine
Cam's Hope, Book Ten

MacLarens of Fire Mountain

Tougher than the Rest, Book One
Faster than the Rest, Book Two
Harder than the Rest, Book Three
Stronger than the Rest, Book Four
Deadlier than the Rest, Book Five
Wilder than the Rest, Book Six

Romantic Suspense

Eternal Brethren, Military Romantic Suspense

Steadfast, Book One
Shattered, Book Two
Haunted, Book Three
Untamed, Book Four
Devoted, Book Five
Faithful, Book Six
Exposed, Book Seven
Undaunted, Book Eight
Resolute, Book Nine
Unspoken, Book Ten, Coming Next in the Series!

Peregrine Bay, Romantic Suspense

Reclaiming Love, Book One
Our Kind of Love, Book Two
Edge of Love, Book Three, Coming Next in the Series!

Contemporary Romance Series

MacLarens of Fire Mountain

Second Summer, Book One
Hard Landing, Book Two
One More Day, Book Three
All Your Nights, Book Four
Always Love You, Book Five
Hearts Don't Lie, Book Six
No Getting Over You, Book Seven
'Til the Sun Comes Up, Book Eight
Foolish Heart, Book Nine

Macklin's of Burnt River

Thorn's Journey
Del's Choice
Boone's Surrender

The best way to stay in touch is to subscribe to my newsletter. Go to https://www.shirleendavies.com/ and subscribe in the box at the top of the right column that asks for your email. You'll be notified of new books before they are released, have chances to win great prizes, and receive other subscriber-only specials.